THE VINEYARD

WHISKEY RIVER ROAD, BOOK 10

KELLY MOORE

Edited by
KERRY GENOVA
Illustrated by
DARK WATER COVERS

TITLE

CHAPTER ONE

ROSE

"ou're not fat. You're pregnant, and Tucker is loving every minute of it. The way he looks at you, girl…well, let's just say, you should be naked around him any chance you get."

"You're so naughty," Missy snorts through the phone. "You've been in Salt Lick way too long. I bet you haven't found a cowboy to do the boot-scootin' boogie with you since you moved back."

"The cobwebs do need to be dusted off." I sip on my coffee as I enjoy my morning on the outside deck of my bistro, admiring the rolling hills before I open the winery for the day.

"You could always come for a visit to Lexington.

We have a hot new neighbor who bought the land adjacent to us."

"I may just have to do that if my dry spell doesn't break soon. Seems like all the men here are either married or have no ambition."

"Your problem is you have pretty high standards when it comes to men."

"True, but if my girlie parts don't get any attention soon, I may have to settle for the cute ranch hand my daddy hired a few days ago."

"At least he's pretty to look at." By her tone, I can almost hear Missy lift her shoulders.

"There is that. Let me know how your doctor's appointment goes today. Tell Tucker I said hello."

"I will. See you soon." She disconnects the line.

In the distance, I see a fancy silver sports car blowing up dust headed down the long dirt drive to the winery. It's too early for customers, probably someone who got turned around and needs directions. Finishing my coffee, I reach into my bag and take out a tube of pink lipstick, applying it to my dry lips. I pay no attention to who gets out of the car as the wind picks up, blowing my fiery-red hair over my shoulders.

"As I live and breathe, if it ain't Rose Methany," a

deep and somewhat familiar voice says, moseying toward me.

Raising a finger, I push my sunglasses down my nose a quarter of an inch to see who's walking up the deck.

"I should've known by the name on the sign." He points. "A Rose By Any Other Name Winery. Isn't that Shakespeare or something?"

A cheeky grin tugs at the corners of my lips. "I'm surprised a city boy like you knows such things."

He pulls out the ornamental wrought iron chair across from me and sits. "Romeo and Juliet, am I right?" He smiles.

"If you can quote the rest of the line, I'll buy you a bottle of my best wine." I lean my elbows on the table.

"That isn't saying much being you own the place, but I'll play along." He taps a finger to his lips. "A rose, by any other name would smell as sweet."

"Dang, you're good." I giggle. "It's been a while since you've been around these parts. I heard you went back to California with some swanky billion-dollar company." My insides are all tingly looking at his fine body and chiseled clean-shaven chin sporting a square dimple right in the middle of it. He ain't the boy I remember. He's all man and much hotter than I recall.

"I was recruited into an investment firm. The billions didn't come until after they hired me." He rolls up his tightly pressed sleeves while sporting a smug smirk.

My pearly pink nail clicks on my sunglasses as I push them back up. "Well, it looks good on you, so does the arrogance." I'm thankful the dark tint on my shades doesn't let him see me staring at his package.

"That's saying a lot coming from you. I thought you preferred a man with a Stetson." He inches his chair closer. "It ain't arrogance, gorgeous. It's confidence."

Leaning back, I cross my long legs and watch as he admires me. "I didn't say I didn't. I just said the city boy look fits you." He's hot as heck in his white button-down and slacks. His shoes are a bit too shiny for me. I prefer the dusty look on a pair of well-worn boots wrapped around my waist.

"This is really all yours?" He glances around.

"Yep, all mine."

"I'm impressed, not that I haven't seen better in Northern California wine country. But, I will hold you to your best bottle of wine for my knowledge of Shakespeare."

"Cocky as ever I see." I stand. "Do you want a tour? Maybe I can change your mind."

"After you." He holds out his hand.

"Don't even pretend to be a gentleman." I laugh.

"Aw, that hurts." He feigns pain covering his heart.

I raise the glass garage-style door opening up the bistro. "We serve crackers and dips made by the locals. Fruit and meat trays too. There are three sandwiches on the menu and two types of salads. Everything here is produced in Salt Lick."

He picks up a bottle of white wine on the counter. "This too."

"Our second year of crops won't be ready for another couple of months. This one specifically was imported from a winery in France that I interned at for a summer. But, I do have bottles in storage from my first crop." He follows me through the building into the winery.

"How did you manage to have a product your first year open?"

"My family planted as per my guidance while I was in France so it would be ready for opening day. They've been working on it for almost two years." I flip on the switch at the top of the stairs and head down the wooden steps.

"I'm sure the next batch will be better," he snarks, following me.

"Who said there was anything wrong with the first one?" My feet hit the floor, and I turn toward him, propping my hands on my hips.

"I've researched it. A fine wine takes time." He flips my hair over my shoulder, heating my body up.

Biting my bottom lip, I turn to one of the barrels, grab a small plastic cup off the shelf and flip the handle on the barrel, allowing no more than a swallow to fill the cup. Holding it up, I say, "Mister, I Know Everything City Boy, tell me what you think."

His hand brushes with mine as he takes it from me, and I hear him inhale, and his eyes darken. He's as turned on by me as I am him. I lick my lips when he places the wine to his. He tilts his head back, savoring the taste as his Adams's apple bobs, swallowing the wine.

"Downright perfection," he purrs, with his gaze roaming my body.

I close the gap between us. "The wine, or me?" I whisper against the corner of his mouth, then press mine to his. I taste the blueberry sweetness of the wine.

He pushes his tongue past my lips for a quick taste. "I like that you chose blueberries as opposed to grapes."

"I have crops of both." I stare into his heated eyes.

He tosses the cup to the ground, freeing his hands, and grasps my hips, pulling me closer. I shed him of his shirt as he inches up my dress, finding me bare.

"Damn, woman," he hisses, backing me up against the barrel. He weaves his hand up my dress to my breast, squeezing my nipple. "These are perfect too." His teeth graze my neck.

I know I'm going to regret this, but I can't stop myself. It's been far too long since a man has touched me as if he wants to eat me alive. I rip his belt from its loops and unzip his pretty britches. Cupping him, his warm breath blows against my skin. At this point, I don't think he can stop any more than I can, nor does he want to.

He hikes my leg over his hips and lifts me, plunging inside me. My head falls back and my hair catches in the cracks of the barrel. I don't let it interfere with what we're doing. It's wrong on so many levels, but it feels so darn good. He delves further inside, and the rough wood of the barrel scrapes my back. I dig my nails into his shoulders to keep from moving up and down. I can't stop the reaction my body has to his movements. He's either really good, or it has been too long. I bite the inside of my cheek to keep my moan inside. He bolts his hips up one more time, and he lets go. He pants as he braces against my body for a moment before we both go to the floor.

"I'm sorry," he says, looking down.

I place my hands on either side of his face, forcing him to look into my eyes. "For what?"

"I didn't use a condom."

"No worries, I'm on the pill. Have been for many years."

"Still, it wasn't very gentlemanly of me."

I push him off and stand. "Nothing you just did would be considered honorable." I adjust my dress. "I ain't complaining or nothing."

He gets off the ground. "I've always been attracted to you," he says, zipping up his pants.

"Well, now that we've gotten that out of our systems, we can continue the tour of the winery." I act like it meant nothing as I climb the stairs, and he follows as he buttons his shirt.

We walk through the vineyards and I tell him about each type of blueberry and grape I've grown. Every now and then, I look behind me and he's watching my ass sway. Suddenly stopping, he runs into me. "Why are you here, Dodge? I know you didn't come this far for a quickie with me." I brush my pink lipstick from his bottom lip.

"To be truthful, I'm interested in purchasing your company."

I laugh. "It ain't for sale." I march past him, heading back into the barn-style building.

He's on my heels. "Everything has a selling price, Rose."

When I reach the door, I whirl around, pointing a finger at his chest. "I said it ain't for sale!"

"The men I work for really want to purchase it. You've created quite a market in a short period of time. They're willing to pay double what it costs you to build it."

I feign interest. "Double you say." I bat my eyes.

"Yes, and you'd be smart to take it."

My blood boils. To think, just a few minutes ago my blood boiling was something good. Now it's done pissed me off. "You can tell your partners to go to hell. This is my life. I won't be selling to anyone, much less the likes of you! How could you? You acted like you didn't know I owned this place!"

"Don't be like that, Rose." He reaches out to touch me, but I swat his hand away.

"Don't think what we just did will ever happen again. Go back to California and tell them my business is not for sale. Not now, not ever!" I slam the door in his face.

"I'm such an idiot. A gorgeous man looks at me with puppy dog eyes, and I give in way too easily." I toss my sunglasses on the counter and storm into the bathroom. My hair is a total mess, and my is neck is as red as my curls from his mouth being pressed against it. "I'm such a stupid woman when it comes to men." I splash water on my face. "My standards don't seem to be too high now, do they, Missy?" This is why I prefer a one-night stand. I'm not the marrying kind, and I don't believe in true love. My daddy would beg to differ with me. He says he's loved momma from the first day he laid eyes on her. I have to admit, they are happy.

Drying my face, I make my way back to the cafe table on the deck where I left my phone. I pick it up, and it starts vibrating. It's Tucker. "Good Lord, did Dodge tell him what we just did?" I hesitantly answer it.

"I don't know what he told you, but—"

"Calm down. Who's he?" he interrupts.

"Dodge. He showed up here out of the blue trying

to get me to sell my winery to him." And get in my panties…well, that's if I owned any.

"Dodge is in town?"

"He didn't call you?"

"No, he didn't."

"I'm sure you'll hear from him soon. Why are you calling?"

"To tell you that I'm going to surprise Missy and bring her out to the ranch for the weekend. It's been awhile since we came for a visit, and I know she'd love to see you. She mentioned the band you hired to play at the vineyard."

"Oh, I'd love to get her on stage."

"I think you could convince her to sing, that is if she can get past feeling like a bloated watermelon. Those are her words, not mine. I think she's sexy."

"She's a lucky woman to have you. Why can't your brother be more like you?"

"What's he done to piss you off other than wanting to buy your business? I'd take that as a compliment. He's become a business tycoon."

"He's still an ass," I mutter, and he chuckles.

"I'll call him and tell him to apologize for whatever he's done to you."

"No need, I done took care of it." I don't want him and Missy to know we bumped monkeys in the cellar. I'll have to keep my horniness in check whenever I'm around him. He's so much sexier than the last time I saw him. Those chocolate-colored eyes have specs of gold in them that are mesmerizing. Gah, the feel of his biceps under my grip has me pressing my thighs together.

"So, don't let on to Missy when you talk to her."

"I won't." I shake it off, recalling what we were talking about and watch into the distance as Dodge turns out of the long drive headed toward town.

"Guess who's beeping in?" Tucker says.

"I'm guessing your brother. Please don't mention we talked."

"Catch you later, Rose."

Flipping on all the lights, I march behind the polished pine counter to research Dodge. I haven't thought about him in years. I can't believe I gave in to him so easily. Googling investment firms in California, it isn't long before I find his handsome face plastered on the company's page. It brags about him purchasing up-and-coming companies and turning them into a gold mine. Tucker's right. I should take it as a compliment, but it pisses me off instead. I've invested and dang near borrowed from everyone I know to get this place up and running. In the first year, I've paid off almost all my debt other than the land. Daddy says it's a gift, but I fully intend on paying him back one day. He and Momma have done enough for me. They paid my way through college. I can never repay them the debt of taking me in when my grandmother died. Not for one second of one day have either one of them ever not treated me as if I wasn't one their own. Thanks to them, I have a great life, and a brother I adore. It's hard to believe River will be five years old in a couple of months. If Daddy wouldn't have found me, Lord knows what kind of trouble I would've gotten myself into. I know for sure, I wouldn't be the person I am today.

I read the article on Dodge. It never once mentions him being from Kentucky. It's as if they glossed over it, and his life didn't begin until he went to college in California. Maybe they didn't think some small-town country boy would be good for their reputation. Funny, I'd like him more if he'd go back to his roots instead of trying to be something he's not. Missy said the year after they got married, when I was away at college, Dodge would come help at the ranch. He's good with the horses. She said a few times he'd gotten so comfortable he'd let his southern drawl spill out.

One thing about me, I ain't never been embarrassed of my roots even when I was told I'd do better to lose my accent when I was meeting with more upscale vineyards. If people don't like me for who I am, I ain't got time for them. It made me more determined to be successful. Daddy always taught me to be true to myself, work hard, and to be honest. I've found it to work in my business life. Too bad my personal life doesn't work the same way. He'd be darn tootin' mad at me if he knew that I wasn't…let's just say… less than virginal.

CHAPTER TWO

BOONE

"*H*ow's my favorite daughter?"

"Lord, Daddy! You scared the bejesus out of me!" Rose jumps, covering her hand over her chest.

"You must've been lost in thought if you didn't hear my boots scuffing up the floor." I chuckle.

She closes her laptop. "I was just doing some research before customers start walking in the bistro." She glances at her watch. "I have a fresh pot of coffee. Would you like some?"

"Wouldn't mind a cup." I join her behind the counter. "Was that Dodge Anderson I saw turning out of the drive?"

"Yes, it was. He showed up here this morning out

of the blue." Her face flushes as she grabs a black coffee mug from under the counter, filling it.

"What's that on your neck?" I point to a red mark.

She covers it with her hair. "Nothing. I must've scraped it on something when I was checking the wine barrels this morning."

"Looks more like someone had their teeth to your skin." I hold in my laughter, knowing I'm making her uncomfortable. As much as I don't like it, Clem has told me our feisty daughter has a bit of a wild side when it comes to men.

"What are you doing here this early? Don't you have some cattle wrestling to do or something?" She tries to quickly change the subject.

"You have a shipment coming in this morning. I thought I could give you a hand with it."

"You're always helping me out around here. I appreciate it." She snags a cookie from a glass jar, handing it to me. "It's your favorite."

"Are these Nita's peanut butter cookies?"

She nods.

"You better make sure your grandpa doesn't get ahold of these. He'd stash them from Winnie." I laugh.

"Poor Grandpa. She keeps him on a pretty strict

diet since his heart attack." She takes out a towel and wipes down the countertop.

"Not as strict as she thinks."

"At least he's given up those nasty smelling cigars."

"Don't kid yourself. He hides out in the barn way too often."

"I'll box up a few of these cookies for River. Where is he? You usually bring him out so he can pick some blueberries."

"He had a belly ache this morning, so I left him with his momma."

"Oh, maybe these cookies ain't such a good idea." She stops filling the box.

"I'll take some to the men." I indicate with my finger for her to keep piling them in the box.

"You ain't kidding no one. I know exactly who's tummy these will be filling." She giggles.

"Ellie was reviewing the books last night, and she said you've done so well that we can expand the crops for next year and add on an additional area to store the bottled wine. She thinks you need to expand into the international market. You've got enough contacts you could grow it three hundred percent."

She leans her elbows on the counter. "I was thinking the same thing."

"I'd like to say great minds think alike, but we're talking Ellie here. That could be dangerous." I smirk.

"Oh, Daddy, you know you love her, and she's as smart as a whip."

"Yeah, with a touch of crazy," I snort.

She taps a finger to her temple. "I may just know someone who could expand my sales into the international market."

"Who?" I sip my coffee.

"I'm going to keep that information under my hat for now. It's going to take some planning to change the person's mindset."

I laugh. "That means you're going to use your womanly persuasiveness on a man."

"What would you know about such things?" She props a hand on her hip.

"Darling, don't think for one minute your momma was all sweet and innocent."

She hops up on the counter. "This I have to hear. Do tell."

Placing my mug on the counter, I walk over to her and kiss her cheek. "I kinda like my balls where they set. If I shared some of the things she did to win

18

me over, they'd likely be hanging from the back of my truck."

She howls out in laughter. "You're a big rugged cowboy who's never backed down from a fight, but you're scared of Momma."

"She ain't right." I wink.

She jumps down, throwing her arms around me. "I hope one day I have a love like yours and Momma's," she admits even though I've heard her say she don't believe in true love.

"I want that for you with a good man."

She loosens her grip from around my waist. "In your mind, will there ever be anyone good enough for me?"

"You make a good point." I chuckle. "He'll have to prove himself."

"Yeah, to you and every Calhoun in the family," she snickers.

"Missy found a good man in Tucker, so it's possible." I pick up my coffee. "Just stay away from the likes of his brother."

Her brows scrunch together. "What's so wrong with Dodge?"

"I've heard conversations between him and Tucker. He's money hungry and hasn't always been on the up and up with the way he works. You need a hardworking cowboy. Not a man who loves money more than he would a woman. You're an independent young lady who has worked smart and hard to build a future for yourself."

"Doesn't that make me money hungry too?" She tilts her head to the side.

I rinse out my cup in the sink. "Answer me this, is money the most important thing in your life? Would you trade it for your family?"

"Of course not," she huffs, "but I'd fight like heck to keep this place, just like Grandpa has done for the ranch."

"Exactly. For his family, not the money. Dodge Anderson ain't that kind of man."

"Well, then good thing I ain't lookin' for love with Dodge." She steps on her tiptoes, kissing my chin.

Over her shoulder, I see a delivery truck pull up. "You open up business. I'll help unload the supplies."

"Thanks, Daddy."

"Love you, darling." I shuffle off to direct the driver to go around back. Before I start offloading the boxes, I call Clem.

"How's River? Feeling any better?"

"He's running a fever now, and he says his head hurts so bad he doesn't want to open his eyes."

"Maybe you should call Doc."

"I already have. He's going to meet me in his office in an hour."

I glance at my watch. "I'll be finished here in thirty minutes. I'll meet you at his office."

"Thanks, I'd like that. River hasn't been sick a day in his life and I'm a little nervous." Her voice cracks.

"It's probably some virus. Ellie's kids all had colds last week and he hung out with them."

"I'm sure you're right."

"I gotta go if I'm going to get done in time." I hang up and stack a couple of the boxes to carry into the storage area. It doesn't take long before the truck is unloaded, and I've updated the inventory log.

When I walk around the front of the bistro, there are several cars parked out front and a few tables are already filled. Rose is working behind the counter, wearing a white apron. "Your help didn't show up this morning?" She hired a young lady that she went to high school with. Unlike Rose, she stayed in Salt Lick and married one of our ranch hands. Sweet girl and a hard worker.

"Lacey took the morning off. She worked yesterday, and we were so busy she stayed late."

"I'd offer to stay and help, but I'm meeting your momma and River at Doc's place."

Her face fills with concern. "He must really be sick."

"I'm sure he's fine."

"Give him a kiss for me. I'll call later to check on him."

"If it gets too busy for you to handle, call Jane. She's offered to lend a hand anytime you need it."

"I'll be fine after the morning crowd dies down."

"I'll catch you later," I say, hustling to my truck.

* * *

"I WANT you to keep a close on eye him. If his fever worsens, call me, and I'll meet you at the hospital," Doc is saying as I walk into the exam room.

"What's going on?" I squeeze Clem's hand and ruffle River's thick dark hair.

"Doc says he's got the flu." Clem's eyes look tired and worried.

"The only reason I'm letting him go home is because of your medical knowledge. You need to keep him hydrated and make sure he gets lots of rest. I'm going to have my nurse come in and draw some blood just to be sure there isn't anything else going on."

"Like what?" I question.

"I'm just being cautious with Clem's history," he mutters, as he writes on a prescription pad. "This will help with his bellyache." He hands it to Clem.

I gather River in my arms, and the heat coming off him soaks into me. "Damn, he's really hot. Are you sure he wouldn't be better off in the hospital?"

Doc stuffs his pen in his white jacket pocket. "I can admit him."

"No. I want to take care of him at home. If I feel I can't handle it, I'll call you like we talked about." Clem brushes the hair off River's forehead. "The hospital can be a scary place for a child. He'll do better at home."

"Call my cell phone when you get the lab work back," I say, pushing open the door with the toe of my boot. I buckle him in his booster seat in Clem's truck. "I'll meet you back at the house."

"You have work to do. The cattle have to be driven to the backside of the property," Clem says, climbing behind the wheel.

"Bear can cover for me. I want to be close by in case little man needs something. I'll run by the store and grab his favorite ice cream for when he's feeling better."

"Ginger ale might come in handy," Clem says.

"Anything you need?"

"Just for my baby to be better."

I lean in the window, kissing her. "With you taking care of him, he'll be good as new in no time."

"Love you, baby."

"Love you, too, doll."

"Well, I declare, Dodge Anderson!" Margret is standing beside the counter at the Magnolia Mill, leaning on a walker.

Jane looks up from the computer. "Look what the cat drug in. You haven't been around here in years." She moves to hug me.

I place my shopping bags on the floor and embrace her. "It's good to see both of you."

"Tucker tells me you've been doing very well for yourself," Jane comments.

"I have."

"You here for a visit?" Margret asks. "I'm surprised you ain't staying in Lexington with Tucker and Missy."

"I'm in town on business."

Jane looks me up and down and then grabs a Stetson out of my bag. "This don't appear to be business attire."

"I thought I might fit in a bit better in a pair of blues jeans and a plaid shirt."

Margret moves with the walker in my direction. "The city boy suit looks good on you. I miss Wyatt all gussied up in his pinstripe suits, but there ain't nothing like a cowboy in tight fittin' jeans and a pair of dusty old boots." She literally purrs.

Jane swats her away. "Don't mind her. Wyatt's been out wrestling cattle for a week."

I laugh. "How have you been? Tucker told me you'd gone through a rough patch a while back." A little girl comes running around the corner holding her hands in the air.

"Momma," she squeaks.

Jane bends down, picking her up and propping her on her hip. "This is my daughter, Mercy."

"Dang, she's a cutie." I tweak her cheek, and she tucks into Jane's shoulder.

"She's the spittin' image of Ethan," Margret says.

I ain't ever been much on kids, but she looks like a little angel. I'll be happy to be Uncle Dodge when my brother's baby pops out, but Daddy is not a role I ever want to play.

Jane walks behind the counter, setting Mercy down. "How long you needing a room for?"

"Do you have anything available for a month?"

"Only the best suite in the house, but it'll cost a pretty penny." Margret moves to a chair and sits.

I pull out my credit card. "No problem," I say, handing it to Jane.

"You been by to see Rose?" she asks, swiping my card.

Have I seen Rose? I ask myself. Her pretty pink nipple rolling between my teeth comes to mind, not to mention the feel of her legs wrapped around my waist. The smell of her skin and the touch of her hand on my bicep.

"Earth to Dodge." Jane is waving the credit card at me with a smirk.

"Yes, I've seen Rose," I finally answer. "She's built herself quite a future with her vineyard."

"We're all very proud of her," Margaret states.

"Without a doubt." If she tells her family what I'm up to, they'll run me out of town with a barrel of a shotgun. I've got my job cut out for me if I want to get my hands on her business and not get myself killed by a Calhoun. I'll have to gain her trust, so she'll never know what happened. It's really too bad. She's kinda like family, and the fact that I truly do like her spunk, not to mention she's gorgeous. In the past, it's been easy to persuade the ladies to sell me their businesses. I have a feeling Rose will be my biggest challenge.

"You're all set. Take the stairs to the top floor, and it's the second door on the right." Jane hands me a key.

"Dinner is served at six," Margret chimes in. "Will you be joining us?"

"I'll have to let you know. I'm not sure what my plans are at this moment." I pick up my bags, heading up the polished wooden stairs to the top floor. As I'm unlocking my door, my cell phone vibrates in my pocket. Setting the bags down, I answer it, knowing it's my boss.

"Hey. I'm just getting settled in my room," I tell Jett.

"I thought it was going to be a quick trip there and back."

"This purchase is going to be a bit tougher than I originally thought. It's going to take some time."

"How much time?"

"Maybe a month or so. Besides, I have family here I haven't seen for a while, and I haven't taken any time off since I started with the firm."

"You're right. You deserve it. You've worked hard

and made a fortune for us. Anything you need let me know. I can send backup for you."

"I'm good. The owner will take some convincing, but in the end, she'll sell to me. My brother's first child is due in a month. I want to stick around for it."

"Keep me posted."

"Will do." Before I've disconnected, Tucker's name pops up. He gave me a lot of guff when I called him after leaving Rose's place. "Did you call to chew off more of my ass?"

"Missy said I was hard on you. I called to apologize. It would've been nice knowing you were back rather than hearing it from Rose."

"Let's get something straight right off the bat. I'm not back. I'm here on business, and when it's done, I'll be leaving this one-horse town."

"That city life of yours really has your panties in a wad." He chuckles.

"To each his own, brother."

"I don't think you hate it as much as you protest. When you let your guard down, I've seen you enjoy the ranch."

"Visiting and living here are two separate things," I scoff.

"Will you be staying with us?"

"I checked into the Magnolia Mill for the time being."

"I know I gave you a hard time earlier, but you're welcome to stay with us."

"You and Missy have enough to deal with right now between getting ready to be parents and hitting the training hard with the racehorses. It's breeding season too for the cattle."

"The ranch could always use some extra hands."

"Thanks, but no thanks," I snort. "I don't like getting my hands dirty these days." At least not with cow shit.

"Boy, how you've changed. You used to love riding the horses."

"Well, I grew up and grew out of playing Cowboys and Indians."

"Ouch," he says. "I'd like to think I do way more than what you've described. I love the ranch and the hard work of it. Getting my hands dirty and knowing I've done an honest day's work."

"I take it you don't think my work is honest."

"You've told me about some of the deals you've pulled off, and you justify it by being on the other end of a woman using you, so you know how to play the game."

"I'm sorry I ever mentioned it to you. You really shouldn't throw a drunken conversation in my face."

"Sorry, man. I just wish you'd come back home and ditch the firm. You're better than swindling people out of their dreams for a dollar."

"If it were just a dollar, I'd give it up. Do you realize how many millions I've made in a short period of time." I walk over to the window and draw back the curtain to peer out at the fog lying over the curves of the land

"Is that all you care about? Money?"

"What else is there?" I chuckle.

"The love of a woman, family, and friends, just to name a few."

"You and I are cut from different cloths. A one-night stand with a hot woman is all I need. As far as ever having a family of my own, not in this lifetime."

I hear him blow out a long sigh. "Regardless, I love you, man. I'll be here when life throws you a curveball."

"I appreciate it, but it ain't gonna happen."

"You never answered me earlier. What did you do to tick off Rose?"

"I offered to buy the vineyard. She said no, end of story."

"You do have big cojones. She's got a gold mine

on her hands, and she's worked hard along with the rest of her family. She'll never sell it."

If I can lay on the charm she will. "Rose made that perfectly clear."

"Great. I'd hate for you to make enemies with my wife's family."

"It's all good, man. Trust me." He's going to make my job even harder than Rose.

"I am trusting you. She's family, and not to mention she'll be our child's godmother."

"How is Missy feeling?"

"She's okay. I'm bringing her to Whiskey River this weekend. We can all catch up at the winery. There's a band playing, and Rose is going to try and get Missy on stage."

"Sounds like a plan. I've got some work to do. I'll catch up with you then." I hang up. I should feel awful for what I know I'm going to do while I'm here. Part of me does; the other part likes the challenge. I don't really want to hurt Rose. I'll have to keep my hands to myself when I'm around her, so she doesn't feel like she's lost me along with her business. It's really too bad because if there was any woman in this world I could fall for, it would be her. I've known it since the first day I laid eyes on her in the back seat of my brother's truck. She hated me almost instantly. I did wear her down over time. The attraction has always been between us, but I can't say she's ever fully liked me. My job of screwing her over sure isn't going to help.

I take the stairs back down two more times before I have all my things settled. Pulling out my laptop, I search Rose's winery like I have many times. I go to the about page and see her picture. "Damn, why do you have to be so darn gorgeous?" I trace the frame of her face with my fingertip. "You just may be the one that breaks my heart," I whisper. Clearing my throat, I go back to work, trying to find what I need to convince her to sell to me. I could open up her sales into an international market and it would skyrocket. I read through the reviews on her wine. She really has surpassed any sales I've ever seen in a newer market. All her wines have excellent ratings. Far superior to her competition in the US market. Who would have ever thought little old Rose would take the world by surprise in a competitive industry? Luck has been on her side with the Calhouns. She's come a long way from living in a beat-up trailer with her grandmother to the woman she's become today.

I rest back in my chair with my hands clasped together and my pointer fingers pressed against my lips. "I admire her. She's taken the time to get her education, travel overseas to gain experience and knowledge in all the right places." How can I take that away from her? "Because I'm a bastard, that's how." I stand abruptly, tipping over my chair. I change out of my suit and into clothes that I no longer feel comfortable in but will serve their purpose. After buckling my belt, I lean over, tugging on my boots. Grabbing my Stetson, I stand in front of the mirror, placing it properly on my head. It brings me back to my teenage years when I thought this is what I'd be wearing the rest of my life. I miss the feeling of belonging. I haven't had it since our father took off with Tucker. I used to feel jealous of my brother, all the time he spent with our father. My anger toward my father gave me a different direction in life. One I'm not always proud of, but here I am. I have lots of money to show for it. I don't need or want anything else. At least that's the mantra I've told myself.

Locking the door behind me, I head down to the lobby and run into Ethan and Mr. Calhoun.

"Jane was just telling me you were staying here." Ethan shakes my hand.

"She says you're here on business." Mr. Calhoun's

voice is gruff. He has never been overly friendly to me.

"Yes, sir, and some family time."

He grips my shoulder. "Family is important, son. Don't ever forget it."

"This coming from the man who's run his own daughter off with a shotgun," Jane snorts.

"Sometimes family deserves a swift kick in the…"

"Papa," Mercy squeals when she sees him, running toward him.

"There's my girl." The gruffness in his tone completely melts away as he plants a big kiss on her cheek.

"She has you and her father completely wrapped around her little finger." Jane laughs.

"That's my job, ain't it?" She hugs his neck.

"I've got an errand to run," I say, trying to run out.

"Don't forget dinner later. I'm making a pot of beef stew with homemade biscuits," Margret yells.

My stomach growls at the thought of a home-cooked meal. "Count me in," I say, skating off.

CHAPTER FOUR

CHET

"*H*old up, son!" I'm winded by the time I catch up with Dodge.

"Are you alright?"

He looks at me oddly while he unlocks his sports car. "Yeah, yeah, I'm fine. I could use a ride home." I wave my hand in the air.

"Didn't you come with Ethan?"

"Yes, but he's staying for a bit, and I have some chores that need getting to."

"I was on my way to…you know what, never mind. Hop in." He presses a button, unlocking the driver-side door.

Peering inside first, I try to figure out how I'm going to hunker down to fit in the seat. Standing sideways, I grab onto the roof and squat low, hearing my old bones creak, and scrunch inside with a few moans. "Why don't you get a real man's car? You know, like a truck."

"Have you ever ridden in one of these babies, Mr. Calhoun?" He's all smiles.

"I can't say that I have." I click the button on my seat belt and make sure it's snug.

"You're in for a treat." He starts the engine.

"I highly doubt it," I mumble.

He backs out then lays the pedal down. My truck handles the dirt roads, and potholes well. This tin can doesn't. He has me bouncing all over the place and gripping the dashboard. "You keep driving like a lunatic, and it ain't gonna be my heart that does me in," I growl.

"Sorry." He slows his speed.

"What did you say has you staying in Salt Lick rather than with your brother?" He's up to something, and I intend to find out what it is.

"I'm here on business."

I scratch my scruffy whiskers. "Tucker told me you buy companies."

"Yes, sir."

"You mean to tell me your highfalutin company out of California is interested in business in our small town? If you have your sights on my land, you can forget it."

"As great as your ranch is, sir, it's not the type of company we purchase. We look for up-and-coming businesses that have potential to skyrocket in sales."

I ain't no idiot like he thinks. He's after the vineyard. That place is the only gold mine in Salt Lick. "Well, then you need to move on. Ain't no place here but ranchers."

"You'd be surprised." He chuckles.

The boy needs to remember what hard-working people do every day to be successful. Blood, sweat, and tears grow a man, not stealing someone else's dream. I think I might be the perfect person to teach him a hard lesson. "Pull over," I order as he drives through the middle of town.

"I thought I was taking you home?" He swerves into a parking spot.

"We have to make a pit stop first." I point to Nita's cafe. "Inside there are the best peanut butter cookies you'll ever put in your mouth." I take out my wallet and hand him cash. "Get a dozen."

"You want me to go in and get them?"

"Nita has strict instructions from my wife to not sell me any cookies. She says they're bad for my heart."

He laughs. "I don't want any part of pissing your wife off."

I square my body toward him, glaring at his face. "You'd rather tick off a man like me? I not only know where all the bodies are hidden, I ordered them removed."

He swallows hard and unbuckles, scampering out.

"Not a word as to who they are for," I holler, and snicker to myself. "That was way too easy."

A few minutes later, he returns with a heavenly smell, handing me the box. "You're welcome," he snarls.

Opening the lid, I take one out and it melts in my mouth.

"Are you at least going to offer me one?" he asks.

"Nope."

He shakes his head with a grin covering his face. "Missy says you're a teddy bear at heart. I'm thinking more like a grizzly."

"It all depends on who I'm dealing with."

"You don't like me much, do you?"

"The jury is still out. Depends on what you're really up to. If you're here to spend time with Tucker and Missy and hang around until they have my great-grandchild, then I'd say that's honorable. But, if you're eye is on making waves with my feisty redheaded granddaughter, well then, the answer is no."

His jaw flexes as he grips the wheel turning onto Whiskey River Road. He jerks the car to miss a deep pothole, and dirt flies so thick he can't see the road. "You ever think about maybe fixing the road?" He slows to a stop, letting the wind carry away the sand.

"This is why real men drive trucks." I bite into another cookie.

When it clears, he doesn't say another word until he parks at the main house. "It's been a...pleasure, Mr. Calhoun."

"I ain't done with you yet, boy. I'm an old man, and I'm needing help with a few chores."

"Don't you have ranch hands for that sort of thing?" He sneers.

"They're all out wrestling cattle today, and the chores won't wait." I motion for him to get out of the car. I don't really need his help, nor do I have any chores left undone, but I'll find something for him to do.

He mouths a few choice words before he climbs out of his tin can.

"You might want to lose the plaid shirt. You're gonna get dirty."

He unbuttons, shrugging it off, leaving his white shirt.

"Is that Dodge Anderson?" Winnie says, coming through the screen door of the house, headed straight toward him for a hug. "It's so good to see you."

I toss the box of cookies in his back seat.

"Thanks, ma'am. Good to see you too."

"Missy didn't mention you were in town."

"It was a surprise."

"Enough chitchatting. The boy has work to do," I say, sternly.

Winnie's head tilts in confusion, and I give her a scowl to keep her from yapping. "I'll just go inside and make you boys some ice-cold lemonade for when you're all done."

I walk up the steps before she can walk through the screen door and whisper against her cheek. "I'll explain later."

I turn around, and Dodge is whipping off his hat, wiping his brow. "Why's it got to be so damn hot here?"

"You've been out of the country for too long, boy." I march past him, headed to the hen house. I grab a wheelbarrow and a shovel. "Since Missy has been gone, this place hasn't been cleaned properly.

With my back aching like it does, I can't do the job justice."

He mutters as he takes the shovel from my hand. I prop a boot up against the barn wall and take out a cigar I sneaked out of the house before I left with Ethan, and light it up. I watch as Dodge gets to work.

"You like the city life?" I ask.

"It beats scooping up chicken shit," he says.

"You got you a lady friend back home?"

"I've been too busy making a career for myself for anything serious."

"A good woman is worth more than any amount of money you can make. Sure they can be a pain in the ass, but it's awful nice to have someone to lay next to at night. Money can't do that for you."

"No, but it can't break your heart either," he says, as he continues to toss chicken poop into the wheelbarrow.

"I've been fortunate enough to have the love of two good women in my lifetime. My Amelia saved me from myself and gave me something I thought I'd never have."

He stops, leaning on the stick end of the shovel. "What's that?"

"My children. There is nothing better than having a family. There were times we didn't have a pot to piss in, but we had each other, and it made all the hard worthwhile."

"It would've been easier if you had money first."

"I suppose, but then my kids would've missed out on something very important in life."

"How to get their hands dirty and smell like chicken shit." He laughs.

"No, the value of hard work and supporting one another no matter what."

"I grew up on my father's ranch like your kids did. He left the hard work to the ranch hands and took off with my brother, following the horse races. I hated ranching. My mother loved it and my father hated it. It's what tore them apart." He gets back to shoveling.

"Tucker tells me you're good with the horses. A man can't hate something and be good at it too."

"I'd have to differ with you. I'm good at my job, but I don't necessarily like it."

"You must like some part to it?"

"I like the challenge of getting people to sell to me."

"I think if you dug down deeper and weren't so stuck on money, you'd find you like ranching. Besides, there is money to be made. Look how well your brother and Missy are doing."

"Yeah, but they are married to the land. People weren't born to live in one place. You can't experience life that way."

"So, the one thing you're angry at your father for is that he couldn't stay at the ranch. He needed more."

He rests the shovel against the chicken wire and narrows his gaze at me. "I never said I was angry at my father."

"You didn't have to say it. It's obvious."

"Look, Mr. Calhoun…" He steps toward me, and my old rooster comes out of the hen house and pecks at his leg. "What the…" He jumps back, and the rooster goes after him.

I whistle loudly and the rooster stops. I lean down, and he gets on my shoulder, facing Dodge and cackling.

"It's alright, boy, he wasn't gonna hurt me."

"That's something I ain't ever seen before." He lowers his hands from his face.

"When you take care of animals, they protect you. If Missy were here, you wouldn't be able to step foot in the chicken pen."

He walks by me, opening the pen door. "Where do you want me to empty the wheelbarrow?"

"In the compost heap." I point in the general

direction. He finagles the wheelbarrow out of the door as I hold it open. He dumps it and rests it against the barn.

"Thanks for the chat. I'll be heading out now."

"There's more work to be done."

He lifts his wrist, glancing at his high-dollar watch. "I really have someplace I need to be."

"Not smelling like chicken shit." I grab his shoulder turning him around to walk with me. "With the men out wrestling cattle, there's been no time to clean the horse stalls."

He stops dead in his tracks. "You want me to clean up horse shit, too?"

"You already stink." I hand him a shovel.

"Can we just skip the work, and you give me whatever lecture it is you're wanting to tell me?"

"No lecture. I'm an old man who needs a hand." I could work circles around this boy.

"Fine." He pushes open a stall to one of our mares ,who hasn't been broken. Walking straight up to her, he pats her mane. "You're a beauty," he tells her.

It's the first time I haven't seen her buck up and run to a corner. I watch him as he continues to talk to her. He reaches down, picking up a carrot out of her bucket, and hand-feeds her. "You're such a sweet girl."

"Huh," I remark.

"What?" he grumbles, as he picks up a rake and works the hay in her stall.

"She ain't friendly to anyone, and you walk right in smooth-talking her. Your brother is right. You do have a way with horses. I'd argue with you about not liking ranching, boy."

CHAPTER FIVE

ROSE

he breeze at the end of the day is refreshing, and the sweet taste of blueberries makes it even better. I toss one in my mouth and a handful in my bucket. Harvesting them by machine would be easier, but the quality of the fruit remains its best if they are hand-picked. Besides, I like the manual labor. It comes from being a rancher's daughter.

The breeze changes directions and a stench fills my nose. "What's that smell?" I glance over my shoulder, and Dodge is standing behind me. I stand, taking off my floppy hat. "What the heck happened to you?" He's no longer in his city slicker clothes. His tight white ribbed tank top is drenched in sweat and has brown stains on it. He starts to answer me and I lift my hand. "Wait." Taking a step closer, I lean in. "You're a mixture of horse and chicken poop."

He stares down at his clothes. "Your grandfather…" I stop him again.

"Had an intervention," I howl in laughter.

"What?" He scowls.

"He made you do his chores, didn't he?" I pluck a piece of straw from his thick hair.

"Under the guise he was too old to do them." He brushes his hands down his shirt, trying to rub the dirt off. "My grandfather can outwork any man in Salt Lick. I can't believe you fell for it." I giggle.

"He's a crazy, grumpy, old man," he snarls.

"Whenever he thought one of us either needed a to talk or a lecture, he'd make us do chores and stand over us yammering on about something in his life or teaching us a lesson. He must've seen right through you, thinking you were up to no good."

"Yeah, he kept saying something about money not being the most important thing in life."

I hand him my bucket of blueberries. "Do you know how many of these sweet little babies it takes to make a gallon of wine?"

"I can't say I do."

"I thought you'd done your research." I place my hat back on and start walking down the row of blueberries. "If you want to profit off something, you should know these things. You can't just come in and try to buy something you don't know every detail of."

He walks behind me. "That part is not my concern. I take in expenses and profit and come up with a bottom line."

"You told me yourself you buy up-and-coming companies that will make you lots of money down the road."

"I put together the offer. I have people that work the other end."

"You have people," I snicker. "So, you basically rob people of their dreams and sell it off to the highness bidder."

"You make it sound awful." He frowns.

"That's because it is."

He walks beside me quietly for a moment. "How many?"

I raise a brow. "How many what?"

"How many pounds of blueberries does it take to make a gallon of wine?"

"Fifteen."

He skims the acreage of land. "That's a lot of blueberries."

"Six pounds of grapes."

"How did a sweet, sexy, young woman like you get so smart?"

"I took in everything I could in school, and during my internships abroad. I didn't sleep more than four hours a night for a solid year."

"How come you didn't find a man to marry when you were gone?"

"Who said I didn't?"

He lifts my left hand. "Because there's no ring." He kisses my fingertip.

I jerk my hand away. "Don't be coming on to me. I know why you're really here."

He stares intently into my eyes. "Is there a man you have waiting on you, Rose?"

"That's none of your business." I shrug one shoulder.

He steps closer. "If there is someone, he doesn't deserve you."

I laugh. "I think it would be the other way around, considering you and I did the dirty in the wine cellar."

He rubs a knuckle down my cheek. "We could do it again." His voice is husky.

"That was a mistake, and will not happen again."

His hand trails down my arm, giving me goose

bumps. "I've liked you since the day we met. You're the most intriguing woman I've ever known."

A snort escapes my nose. "Wow, that's not a word that's ever described me before. Country girl with lots of dreams, but not intriguing."

"You are to me."

I'm not going to be sucked in by this smooth-talking tongue. "You're not my type, Dodge. I'm not sure we're even friend material."

"So, I'm the bad boy you just want to screw."

"It was a lapse in judgment, nothing more. It's been a while since I've had sex, and you were way too willing." It's a lie. I do like him, even though I think he's a snake. Shame on me.

"Ouch."

"Sorry." I turn and pick a few more blueberries. "I think you should turn that Corvette of yours around and head back to California. I'm not going to sell you my business."

"What if I want to hang around to get to know you better?"

I spin around to face him. "Stop."

"Stop what?"

"You came here for one thing and one thing only. Our hanky-panky was a bonus for you."

"Fine, what can I do to prove to you I want to stick around for you?"

This is my opportunity to take advantage of him. "Teach me how to grow into the international market."

I can tell he's mulling it around in that head of his because he's gnawing on the inside of his cheek. "Okay."

"Really?" I raise my brows.

"Yes. I'll coach you on it."

My mind rolls with the idea that he's doing it so my vineyard will be worth more and he'll try to steal it from me. I'll play his game, but there's no way on this earth I'll sell to him or anyone else. "Are you willing to shake on it?" I extend my hand.

"No." He grabs me by the waist. "I want to kiss on it."

Placing both my hands firmly on his chest, I push him away. "I done told you, it ain't gonna happen, city boy."

He chuckles. "You'll give in to me at some point."

"Don't count on it." I brush him off. "I will admit, I do like you in a tight pair of jeans much more than them pretty boy slacks." My gaze grazes down his body.

He holds out his hand this time. "I'll help you if we can be friends."

I don't trust him at all. I plan on using him as much as he wants to use me. He may be one sexy man I'll have a hard time controlling myself around him, but I'll outsmart him. "Deal."

"When do you want to get started?"

"On Monday. Tucker and Missy will be here for the weekend. I want to spend every moment I can with them."

"Yeah, he told me they'd be here. It will be nice to see them."

"Good. Then we agree. No shop talk while they're here. It won't be too much longer before the baby arrives. Things will change at that point."

"Better them than me," he mutters.

"You don't want kids one day?"

"I'm not the daddy kind. I have too many things I want to do and places I want to travel in life. A kid would only get in the way."

"Well, I guess it's good you know what you want."

"I'd love to have a woman enjoy those things with me."

"A woman. Not a wife?" I don't know why I'm asking him. I have no desire to be married. That's actually not true. I've dreamed of marrying the perfect man, but after my last relationship, it was a hard lesson learning there is no such thing.

"I'm not the marrying kind."

"You don't want to be married or have children. Sounds a little lonely to me."

"Um, I don't see you having either one."

"You're right. I'm too focused on growing my business."

"Why don't you finish giving me the tour we started earlier?"

"I think maybe we should avoid the wine cellar" I wink.

"We could be friends with benefits." He grins.

I playfully punch him in the shoulder. "Not gonna happen."

"Suit yourself. I'm a willing participant if you change your mind." He holds out his hand, indicating for me to take the lead.

I show him the different types of grapes growing in the vineyard. The property rolls up a hill, and I've used every ounce of land on this side of the property.

"It doesn't look like you have much room to grow." He scans the property turning his head from side to side.

"That's where you're wrong. This land runs adjacent to Uncle Wyatt's property. He's going to lease me a section of his for expansion of growing more fruit."

"Why lease and not purchase?"

"He doesn't want to sell it, and it's a win for him to make more profit. I'll be able to write off the expense of it."

"You should have enough to write off with what you already have."

"I'm planning on doubling the profit next year with the current crop. If I go international, that will triple it, maybe even quadruple it. I'm going to have Uncle Ian start another building to the east of the current one."

"You'll need to hire more hands and become automated."

"I will hire, but I want to stay away from automation. It changes the flavor of the fruit."

"Sounds like you have a good handle on things."

The wind shifts and his stench fills my nose. "Gah, Dodge, you need a shower."

He lifts his shirt to his nose. "Ugh, I stink. We can finish the tour on Monday."

"You could shower at my place if you'd like."

"As tempting as that is, I'm going to eat at the Magnolia Mill. Those ladies know how to cook."

"Are you saying I don't?" I scrunch my nose.

"According to my brother, not so much." He chuckles.

I hate to admit it, but he's right. Momma tried to teach me and I was never really interested. "I can order a mean pizza."

"I eat out a lot. I'll stick to the home-cooked meal. You could join me if you'd like."

"Thanks, but I'm gonna catch up on some reading."

"Where is your place?"

"It's the second story over the cafe. It's not big, but I love the space."

He glances at his watch. "I'd love to see it before I go."

"Fat chance of that. You'd stink up the place." I pinch my nose.

"Monday, then."

We walk back to the main entrance. "Wait here," I say, running up the steps to the cafe. He hasn't moved an inch when I return. "Take this. It's Jane's favorite bottle of wine." My hand brushes his when he grips the bottle. It sends an instant flash of warmth over my skin. I know he feels it too, when his stare is glued to my hand where it touched him. I blow it off. "I'm sure she'll let you sample it."

He raises it in the air. "I'll see you tomorrow with Tucker and Missy."

I roll my eyes. "They'll want to go horseback riding."

"You don't like to ride?" He laughs.

"You'd think me being a rancher's daughter I would, but I've never been as good at it as Missy."

"I'll give you some pointers," he hollers, getting in his fancy car.

Darn it. Why do I like him so much? He's hot, and I'm horny. That's all it is. I'm going to have to hang out with the new ranch hand in order to be able to keep my hands to myself when I'm around him.

CHAPTER SIX

ETHAN

I curl up next to my sleeping wife and kiss the shell of her ear. "Morning, doll."

She stretches like a cat in my arms. "What time is it?"

"It doesn't matter. Mercy stayed at Margret's." I press into her hips.

"You're insatiable." She rolls over, facing me. "You kept me up until all hours of the night, and you're ready to go again." She kisses my chin.

"Are you complaining?" I nip at her nose as my hand cups her beautiful breast.

"No, but my sleep deprivation usually comes from our daughter, not my husband."

"It's not often we have a night without her." I nuzzle the tender skin of her neck knowing it will turn her on. Then I hear a loud growl. I pull back from her. "Was that your stomach?"

"Yes. I'm famished. I was so busy making sure everyone got plenty to eat last night at the bed and breakfast, I hardly had a bite."

I turn to my back, and she snuggles in on my chest. "I think Dodge ate enough for three men." I chuckle.

"Yeah, he said it had been a long time since he had a home-cooked meal." She places a kiss on my collarbone. "We could eat and then come back to bed."

I lift my head, staring down. "What am I supposed to do with this?"

Her hand glides under the sheet and firmly grips my morning wood. She starts to stroke me, and her stomach sounds like a tin can being opened.

My hand stops hers. "This can wait. Let's get you fed."

"Sorry," she says.

I roll out of bed and tug on my boxers.

"Nice tent you have there, cowboy." She glares and throws on one of my t-shirts.

I groan. "I'll go make the coffee."

"I'll see if we have any fresh eggs."

I slap her ass as I follow her into the kitchen, and she yelps. All it does is make me harder.

She swings open the fridge, bends over and looks inside, and I'm graced with a fine view of her ass. "If you don't want me to bend you over the counter and make you scream, you'd better put some shorts on." She peers over her shoulder as I'm adjusting my crotch. She shuts the door and turns, leaning on the fridge, biting her lower lip, and crossing her arms under her breasts. Her nipples are screaming to be tortured by my mouth. I take a step toward her, and she raises her hands.

"Alright, alright, I'll quit teasing you." She giggles. "I need to go to the hen house and get some fresh eggs."

As she tries to scoot by me, I grab her by the back of the neck, hauling her in for a kiss. "Have I told you how sexy you are lately?"

"Repeatedly last night," she says, breathlessly.

"Good, I'm glad you were paying attention."

Her eyes steer downward. "Why don't you go take care of that in the shower while I cook us breakfast?"

"Because I don't want to waste it on nothing. I'll hold out for you."

She squirms out of my arms. "I'll be back in a

dash." She runs into the bedroom and comes out with a pair of skinny jeans on, then heads outside.

Taking two mugs down, I fill them. Picking up one, I meander into my office to check my emails. I've been waiting on a contract to go through to bring in a shipment of cattle for one of the local ranchers who lost almost half their herd to sickness. I was able to negotiate a good deal for him one state over. As I click through my messages, there's an odd one. The heading states, *you'll never see it coming.* Opening it, the only thing on the page is three small dots in a row. I move my cursor to the email address. It's unfamiliar, and when I click the link it goes nowhere.

I hear Jane come back inside. "Hey, where'd you go?" she hollers.

"I'm in my office."

She peeks her head inside. "You okay?"

"Yeah. I'm checking my email. I'll be out in a minute."

"Alright. You have me all worked up. I'm going to scramble a few of these babies, gobble them up so we can pick up where we left off." She rushes out of the room, and I hear pans clinking on the stove.

Using the phone in my office, I dial Wyatt's number.

"Mercy is fine," he says. "Enjoy your day with your wife."

"I plan on it, but I need to know if Rossi has come up on your radar lately?"

"No, nothing new. Why?"

"I got a strange email. I'm sure it's nothing."

"What's your gut telling you?"

"To keep my eyes peeled. Surely he's long forgotten his vendetta against me."

"A man like him never forgets. I think you should trust what you're feeling."

"I don't want to scare Jane for nothing."

"You have security cameras on every inch of your property. The Magnolia has the same."

"Forget it. I'm just overacting. It was probably just spam."

"I'll make some inquires to see if he's been located."

"Thanks, man." I hang up. Sitting back, I clasp my hands together in my lap. I don't want to borrow trouble. Things have been so good here. Our lives are back on track. Jane seems to be better than ever. Between her own counseling and our marriage sessions, life is great. We're stronger than before. Jane has learned to stand and face her issues rather than run. She's a fantastic mother and wife. I'm so glad we decided to work things out rather than giving up. I can't imagine my life without her ever again. But, Rossi's threats will always be a worry. I can't let my guard down where he's concerned. I'll kill him before I ever let him harm my family. Digging the keys out of the back of my desk drawer, I open the gun safe that rests against the wall behind my desk, taking out one of the pistols.

"Did something happen?" Jane's voice comes from behind me.

"No. I just wanted to make sure everything is in its place."

"Your eggs are done," she says, wrapping her arms around my waist from behind me.

Placing the gun back in the safe, I lock it and turn around in her arms. "I think I'm going to take a rain check on breakfast. I need to run to the office and print a contract and run by the Miller's ranch."

"It's Saturday." She pouts. "And, I thought we were going to stay in bed all day."

"I promise I'll be back by midday,and I'll more than make it up to you."

She drops her arms and I let her go. "It's alright. I wanted to check on River. Clem said he's pretty sick. I thought maybe she could use a break."

I follow her into the kitchen. "I'm going to get

dressed. The sooner I get out of here, the sooner I can get back. You eat. I'll grab something in town."

"Feel free to bring home one of Nita's homemade pies."

I stomp off into the bedroom and quickly dress. I hate lying to Jane, but I don't want her frightened. Grabbing my hat from its hook by the door, Jane calls my name. With my hand gripped on the knob, I turn and look at her.

"I love you, cowboy," she beams.

"I love you, too, doll." I want to tell her to keep a watch out for anything unusual, but that would tip her off. "I'll be back soon." Swinging open the front door, I make my way to my truck. It starts up with the turn of my key. As I drive down Whiskey River Road, I call Mike.

"Hey, man. You working today?" I ask.

"Unfortunately, yes. My men are out investigating a break-in last night and I'm covering the office. Why, what's up?"

"Hopefully nothing. Have you gotten anything on Rossi lately?"

"Not since we last heard he was somewhere in Arizona. He managed to escape the authorities there too."

"That was what, a year or so ago?"

"About that. Have you heard from him?"

"I got an email. I wanted to see if you could track it. I know I could've given it to you over the phone, but I didn't want to worry Jane if it was nothing."

"Sure, come in. I'll take a look at it."

"I'm already on my way." Turning off the dirt road, I see Tucker's truck headed my way. He honks when he sees me, and I stop next to him in the middle of the road.

"Hi, Uncle Ethan." Missy waves.

"You two must've left might early to get here."

"Tucker surprised me, so I wanted to spend as much time as I can with everyone. How is Grandpa?"

"Stubborn and cranky as ever." I laugh.

"Is he taking care of himself?" Concern replaces her smile.

"My mother tries to keep up with him, but I think he's abated her a few times."

"I can't wait to see him."

"You seen Dodge?" Tucker asks.

"We had dinner with him at the Magnolia last night. The boy can eat."

He chuckles. "Our mother used to say, he could eat a week's worth of groceries at one sitting."

"Then he hasn't changed a bit." I push the truck

into drive. "I've got an errand to run. I'll catch up with the two of you later."

"Three of us." Missy holds up an equal amount of fingers.

"Three," I repeat. The drive is short, but the town is bustling on the weekend. There's not one open spot in front of Nita's cafe. She's got a gold mine in that place. She's managed it so well she doesn't have to work much at all. She can sit back and enjoy the profits. The police station is two doors down. Mike's SUV is parked out front. He's sitting at the front desk when I walk inside.

"That was quick," he states.

I take out my phone, showing him the email. "You'll never see it coming," he reads it. "You think this is Rossi."

"It was the words he said to me the last time he called me."

He takes my phone and clicks on who sent the email. "It doesn't go anywhere."

"I know. That's why I was hoping you could help me."

He gets on his computer and tries a few things. "I'll have to get our IT guy on it and see if he can make heads or tails of it. In the meantime, I'd play it safe. You need to warn Jane."

"I've got plenty of security cameras on our house and where she works."

"Still, with Rossi, you never know."

"Right, but I'm not going to tell her if this is just some stupid mistake."

"I'll make sure he gets right on this."

"I appreciate it. You know how to reach me if you hear anything." I tap my knuckles on his desk. I don't bother moving my truck; instead, I walk the couple of blocks to the cafe. Molly is standing in line talking on the phone. She smiles when she sees me. "Some handsome cowboy just moseyed into the diner. Yep, he's got dark hair and eyes that sparkle."

"You're talking to Jane, aren't you?" I chuckle.

"I gotta go. I'll call you later. "Hey, Ethan," she says.

"Is there some special running? This place is packed."

"Nita made pumpkin pies. I think the entire town comes out when she posts it on social media."

"They're worth every penny. Where's Noah?"

"He was headed to the main house. He said he had something he needed to see his father about."

"He'll run into Tucker and Missy. They were pulling onto the ranch when I was leaving."

"Oh good. I have a bunch of baby clothes I want to give Missy."

"Between all the Calhoun woman, I don't think she'll want for anything."

"Very true. Speaking of needing something, Jane wanted me to bring a couple of boxes of food over to Clem and Boone's. Poor River isn't feeling good, and they aren't leaving the house."

"I can grab them while I'm here if you want so you don't have to make a trip."

"It's okay. I'm headed to Ellie's. Our kids have a play date. Besides, I want to see if there is anything else they need."

"I'm sure she'll appreciate it." I glance around the restaurant.

"You okay?" She touches my arm.

"Yeah, why do you ask?"

"You seem a little distracted."

"Everything is fine." I pull out my wallet, handing her cash. "I can't wait here forever. Will you snag a pie for Jane?"

"Sure," she says.

"Thanks, Molly."

CHAPTER SEVEN

CHET

"There's my angel." Missy runs into my arms like she did when she was a little girl.

"It feels so good to be home." Her baby bump keeps me from hugging her tight.

"Tucker," I say, holding out my hand over her shoulder.

"Good to see you, Mr. Calhoun."

I let go of my granddaughter. "When you ever gonna drop this mister crap and call me Grandpa?" I draw him in for a quick hug and slap on the back.

"Sorry," he says.

"How you feeling, sweetheart? You look plum beautiful." I drape my arm around Missy's shoulder.

"Ugh, I feel like a New Year's Day float. You know, one of those big blown-up hot air balloons."

"I keep telling her she's gorgeous, but she ain't believing me." Tucker pats her belly.

"I remember when my Amelia felt the same way when she was pregnant with Bear."

"I can't imagine being pregnant four times. I'm thinking one is plenty." She snorts.

"Oh no you don't. We agreed on at least three," Tucker chimes in.

"That was the voice of inexperience. Now that I've been pregnant, I've changed my mind." She cups her hands under her baby bump.

"You can't go doing that," he hollers.

"Well, until you figure out how you can carry the next one, I'm holding out on one." She lifts a single finger.

"Don't you worry, dear. When this little one comes, she'll forget all about the delivery and the last nine months." Winnie comes into the room and kisses Tucker on the cheek.

"She's right," Noah says, walking through the front door. "Molly swore there'd be no more. I think the first one was only a month old when she started talking about having another one." He shakes Tucker's hand and kisses the side of Missy's head.

"Don't you go gettin' his hopes up." Missy playfully swats her uncle in the gut.

"How about we all sit down and enjoy a glass of tea," Winnie says, motioning toward the kitchen table.

"I'd like to join you, but I have to go relieve Wyatt from wrestling the cattle. Margret says she needs him home for a few hours. I stopped by to talk to Daddy in private."

"You sit down and catch up with Winnie. I'll be right back." I follow Noah into my office. Walking around my desk, I sit in my leather chair.

Noah hovers over and opens a rectangular wooden box. "Last time I checked, there were a few cigars in here."

"You here to nag my ass, or did you have something important to say?" My chair squeaks as I lean back.

He chuckles when he sits. "You don't think you have Winnie fooled, right?"

"I think my loving wife gives me some leeway."

"A man stopped by Molly's office the other day, looking to buy some property."

"Stop beating around the bush. Your wife sells real estate that wouldn't be anything out of the ordinary to need to speak to me in private about," I grumble.

"He had his eye on our land."

"I'm reckoning Molly told him it wasn't for sale." The leather creaks when I rest my elbows on the hard wood of my desk.

"She did, but he didn't back down." He pulls a piece of folded paper from his shirt pocket, handing it to me.

I open it, staring at all the zeroes. "That's a hell of a lot of money."

"I told Molly you wouldn't be interested, but she insisted on my showing you the numbers."

I lean back, rubbing my chin. "This money would mean my family could all retire, and so could their children and my grandchildren."

"This land has been in our family for two generations."

"Yes, and I've had to fight to keep it. I'm an old man, and I'm tired."

"You'd seriously consider selling this property?" He's on his feet.

"No. This place will belong to all of you when I'm gone. I don't want one inch of this land to belong to anyone but a Calhoun." I toss the paper on my desk.

"Good. I thought for a minute there you'd consider selling it."

"Money ain't ever meant much to me, but the thought of taking care of my family is appealing."

"You've taken care of all of us all these years. If you want to retire and not work the land anymore, we'll all pitch in more."

Opening a drawer in my desk, I take out a file, handing it to him. "This is how the land will be broken up."

He opens it, reading through it. "You're leaving me the main house?" He glances over the file.

"I am. You never got to love this house like everyone else, except Jane, and I've already spoken to her. She wants you to have it."

"But what about the rest of my siblings?"

"They're all in agreement. The only thing I want from you is a promise to build Winnie a house up on the hill by Amelia's grave. I'll be buried next to her."

"Is that what Winnie wants?"

"Yes, even though she insists she's going to die first." I rap my knuckles on the desk. "As you can see, the acreage is divided amongst all of you. You can either break it down into parcels or keep it all together. I know Wyatt has his own ranch and doesn't want it divided."

"I'm sure everyone else will feel the same way."

"One other thing. The house and the land that Boone and Clem are on will be deeded to them. They'll own all the racehorses. You, Bear, and Ellie will own the cattle."

"What about Rose and Missy?"

"Missy still owns a section of the land where Winnie's house will be built. Rose wants the old run-down farmhouse on the back of the property. She has plans on rebuilding it one day."

"Sounds like you have everything handled."

"I do. So, you tell Molly, to tell whoever this person is to put his sights on someone else's land." I stand.

"I'll be sure to do just that," he says, moving toward the door.

"I'm going to go thoroughly enjoy the day with my granddaughter." I grip his shoulder as we join them in the kitchen.

"Come sit, Grandpa." Missy pats the chair next to her.

"I'm sure we'll all have dinner tomorrow night before you leave town," Noah tells Missy.

"I love when everyone gathers around the table," she says. "Tell Aunt Molly I can't wait to see her."

"I will." Noah walks out.

"How are my chickens?" she asks me.

"Good, but I can't say that old rooster took a hankering to Dodge cleaning out their cage."

"Dodge?" she snorts.

"He ain't ever cleaned out a chicken pen as far as I know." Tucker scratches his head.

"Oh, Grandpa, did you have an intervention? I'm betting Dodge had no idea what he was in for." She giggles.

"I know he's your brother, but I think he's up to no good where Rose is concerned."

"I'll talk to him. Don't worry," Tucker tries to reassure me.

"Rose is more than capable of taking care of herself. She doesn't need the two of you getting in her business." Missy scolds both of us.

"She's right. Rose is smart and she ain't gonna let anyone take advantage of her," Winnie says.

"I'm going to make sure of it. You women can get sidetracked by a handsome face."

Winnie bursts out laughing. "Every one of these Calhoun women are smarter than their men."

"Hey!" Tucker blurts out in defense.

"You men may be the head of your families, but don't you think for one minute the women aren't the neck that makes your heads turn."

"Go, Grandma Winnie." Missy high-fives her.

"You and I will be having a chat later, in private," I growl at my wife.

"Yes, dear." She smiles, refilling everyone's glass.

"Rose should be here anytime. She has someone working the morning shift, so we can go horseback riding."

"Should you be riding in your state?" I ask.

"Oh, Grandpa. I've been on a horse the entire time. You worry way too much."

"Dodge is coming, too, just to give you a heads-up," Tucker adds.

"Who invited him?" I grumble. "My shotgun is still on the porch."

"Be nice. Dodge hasn't been around in a while, and my husband would like to spend time with his brother." Missy runs her hand down Tucker's arm."

"That's fine as long as he don't plan on cozying up with Rose." I point a crooked finger at her.

Missy stands. "We'll all be spending time together this weekend. We're going out to the vineyard tonight. Tucker tells me there's a really good band playing. Would you like to join us?"

She moves beside me. I reach out, holding her hand. "This old cowboy will be in bed by the time the four of you go out."

"What are you talking about? You've always waited up for me to come home."

"The last few years haven't been so kind on my old bones. I'm tired, sweetheart."

She hugs my neck. "Then we'll stay here with you."

"Don't be silly. I want you to go and have a good time. We'll all be together tomorrow. Winnie is planning a feast for the entire family."

"I'll be up first thing in the morning to help," she tells Winnie.

"Jane, Nita, and Ellie will all be here by the crack of dawn," Winnie states.

"What about Aunt Clem?"

"River's been a bit under the weather. I told her not to worry about cooking."

"Nothing serious, is it?" Missy's brows draw together with worry.

"Boone says it's the flu. He'll be alright. Him being sick will keep Clem tied up for a while. She won't want to leave his side."

"There you are!" Rose squeals, running into the house, grabbing Missy into a full-on hug. "I've missed you so much!"

"We've missed you too," Missy says as Tucker embraces both of them.

"Let me see your belly." She pulls back from Missy. "You're right. You look like you're gonna burst at any moment."

"I told you," Missy scolds Tucker.

"Why did you have to go and say that?" He scowls at Rose.

"I didn't say she wasn't as cute as a bug in a rug, but dang girl, you're carrying a watermelon," she snorts.

"I think she's sexy." Tucker jerks her from Rose.

"Now that's what I'm talking about. I done told you he looks at you like he wants to eat you alive." Rose is laughing, and Missy's cheeks are turning the color of a strawberry.

"This is more than my ears want to hear about my granddaughter," I growl.

Dodge walks in, taking off his hat. Missy and Tucker go to his side, and Rose stands back, watching him.

"Mr. Calhoun," his deep voice is directed at me.

"Did you come back to muck the other stalls?" I can't help but put a dig in.

"Leave the boy alone. You four go have fun." Winnie shoos them away and gives me the stink eye.

CHAPTER EIGHT

ROSE

"*D*amn, woman. For someone who doesn't like horseback riding, you sure make a pair of chaps look good." Dodge tugs at my red plaid shirt that's tied up around my waist while his gaze drags down the length of my long legs.

"I'm sure glad to see you appreciate a country girl's ways," I tease. He's smoldering in his tight jeans and dark chocolate t-shirt that brings out the colors in his eyes. His hair's a wavy mess, unlike the kept city boy look he had yesterday when he arrived.

"Here." Missy hands me the bridle of the horse I'll be riding. "You do remember how to ride, right?" She laughs, glancing between the two of us.

I recall what it felt like to ride him. "It's like riding a bike," I say, putting my foot in the stirrup.

Dodge lets out a low, sexy moan as if he read my mind. Dang him. "Let's see you straddle a horse, city boy."

He adjusts his hat, plants a boot in the stirrup and swings his leg over the horse. He's a natural, and darn if he don't look sexier. "Easy as pie." He grins.

Tucker has to help Missy get on the horse because her belly keeps her too far away from the side of the horse. Once on, she's a pro. Tucker follows suit and climbs on his horse.

"I want to ride out to Grandma's grave. I need to tell her all about the baby." Missy gets her horse moving, and we follow.

The area she wants to go to is the furthermost point of the ranch. It sits tall, and you can see for miles. Missy leads, Tucker's in step with her, and Dodge is riding next to me. He's making my heart thump harder than normal. I need a distraction.

"So, I had some thoughts on making the vineyard international."

He chuckles. "What happened to no shop talk this weekend? I wanted things to stay friendly between us."

"You're right. I'm sorry. We should keep things civil for Missy and Tucker's sake."

"Are you saying you think things are going to get heated between us if we work together?"

"First of all, we ain't working together, as you put it. Secondly, if you mention buying the vineyard, then yes, things will get unfriendly."

"Then, if we ain't working together, I'll send you a bill for my time."

I stop my horse. "I don't expect you to work for free, but there are other people I could get in touch with to help me."

"Are you two riding or arguing?" Tucker hollers over his shoulder.

"Riding," I yell the same time Dodge yells, "negotiating."

"Negotiating my ass!" I say, digging my heels into my horse to make him move. Tucker falls back with Dodge, and I catch up to Missy. "I'm glad you're here. We don't spend enough time together anymore."

"I agree. After the baby comes, I'd like it if you took a few days off to come help me."

"I'd love to, but I ain't very good with babies."

"You're better than you think. I recall how sweet you were with River."

"He was a cute little thing." I grin.

"As much as I love our home, I miss this place."

"Are you regretting your decision to move to the Anderson Ranch?"

"No, not at all. My life is perfect. I just miss seeing my family every day."

"Are you still planning on building a house next to Grandma?"

"Eventually, yes. I want a place on this property to leave my children one day. The memories I have growing up here, I cherish."

"Sometimes I miss living here, too, but I like having a place of my own."

"I'm so proud of you, Rose."

"Have I ever thanked you for treating me like your sister? When I moved here all those years ago, I was scared shitless. You made it feel as if I belonged."

"You filled a place in me I needed, too. You are my sister, and I'd do anything for you."

I reach out my hand, and she holds it. "I feel the same way."

"What are you two getting all mushy about?" Tucker laughs.

"Nothing. Mind your own business," I snicker.

We ride up and down the valleys of the land until we make it to the top, where the area flattens out.

"Wow, what a view," Dodge says, scanning the property.

"You've never been up here before?" I ask.

"No, but I'm glad I'm here now."

Tucker helps Missy off her horse. "This is where I'm going to build our cabin." She motions with her hands.

I climb off my horse and walk over to Grandma's headstone. Bending down, I pick up a single flower someone left and hold it to my nose. I didn't ever get to meet her, but part of me feels as if I know and love her through Missy. "Hi, pretty lady," I say.

Missy flops on the ground next to me. "Hey, Grandma. I miss you. I sure wish you could see my big fat belly."

Tucker squeezes her shoulders, standing behind her. "Are you going to tell her?"

"Tell her what?" I glance up.

Missy reaches out and touches Grandma's headstone. "We're having a son."

"Oh, my gosh. I'm so happy for you," I say. "I know Tucker really wanted a boy."

"I'd have been happy either way," he replies.

"I wanted her to be the first person I told." A single tear rolls down her cheek. "To honor both you and Grandpa, we wanted to combine your names. We chose to use your middle name, Morgan."

"I'm sure she'd love that." I grip her hand.

"His full name will be Morgan Calhoun Anderson," Tucker tells her as if she can hear him.

"That's a great name," Dodge states.

"Even if it was a girl, this was the name we picked out together." She tilts her head up to look at Tucker.

"I can't wait for his arrival." He leans down and kisses Missy.

Missy and I spend the next hour telling Grandma about all the things that have been going on in our lives. Somehow I believe she hears us. My heart always feels a little lighter any time I spend time talking to her.

"I need to start heading back," I say, getting off the ground. "I have some set up to do for the band playing at the vineyard tonight." I hold out my hand, helping Missy off the ground.

"I can't wait to see the changes you've made since we were last there," she tells me.

"I'm saving you one of my best bottles of wine to celebrate with once this little one is here." I splay my hand on her belly.

Tucker wraps his arms around her waist from behind. "I'd sure love it if you got on that stage tonight and sang."

"Oh, fat chance. They don't need a whale on stage."

"You're not a whale." He bites the rim of her ear.

"I've already told the band all about you. You're so getting on that stage tonight." I stomp over to my horse.

"Am I invited to come along?" Dodge asks with an unsure look on his face.

"Sure you are. You're family." Tucker slaps him on the back.

Dodge's eyes dart back and forth with mine as if he's asking my permission.

"It will be fun," I say. I'll have to keep my distance from him if he plans on not being in his city boy clothes. Not that it stopped me the first time.

We casually ride down the hills, and just as we make it to the river, my horse starts prancing. "What's wrong, boy?" I try to control him.

I hear the rattle of the snake seconds before my horse bucks and then takes off. "Whoa, boy!" I yell, trying to hold on. He races under a tree, and a branch knocks me off, but my foot doesn't clear the stirrup. I manage to keep my head from hitting the ground, but my shoulder takes several hard licks along with my right side.

I can hear a horse running up behind me. "Whoa!" Dodge says, grabbing the reins. My horse stops on a dime, and I slide out of the stirrup. Before

I can move, Dodge is cradling me in his arms. "Are you hurt?" His hand runs down my body, feeling for broken bones.

I look up, and Missy and Dodge are standing over him. Missy's hand is covering her mouth. "Are you okay?"

"I don't know." I try to lift my arm to rub my head, but instead, wince. "Ouch."

Dodge gently touches my shoulder. "I think it's broken," he says.

"We need to get her to the main house," Missy adds.

"I'll get her horse and tie it to mine. You get her on your horse with you," Tucker directs Dodge.

"No, it's okay. I can ride my own horse." Dodge helps me to my feet, and a wave of pain washes over me, and I feel unsteady.

"You aren't doing anything by yourself." The next thing I know, Dodge has me in his arms again, and he lifts me onto the saddle.

I brace one hand on the leather as he gets on behind me. "Am I hurting you?"

I shake my head. "No."

"I'm going to start out slow. You let me know if it's more than you can stand."

"Okay."

He takes it easy. I don't have the heart to tell him that with every step of the horse, my shoulder throbs. I bite my bottom lip and bear it without a sound.

Tucker and Missy ride ahead to get help. Within a mile of being back, Daddy's truck is tearing up the field heading straight for me.

"What the hell happened?" he barks, jumping from his truck.

"There was a rattlesnake, sir," Dodge tells him. "Her horse got spooked."

"Let me look at her." He gingerly helps me down from the horse. He lifts my chin to look into my eyes. "Did you hit your head," he asks, brushing the hair from my face.

"I don't think so. My shoulder aches, and it hurts to take a breath in."

"You may have fractured some ribs. From the looks of the way you're holding that arm, I don't want to check it out. Let's get you back to the house and let your momma take a peek."

"I don't want to worry her. She's got her hands full with River being sick. Just take me to Doc's place."

"Don't be ridiculous. I was home when Missy came running in. Your momma knows you've been hurt. She'd skin both our hides if we don't come to the house."

"Fine," I mutter. "You okay to ride back on your own?" I ask Dodge.

"Yeah, no problem. I'll meet you at the house."

Daddy helps me get in his truck, and I lean over to try to stave off the pain. He apologizes with every dip of the truck. He drives as slow as he can as he eases to a stop in front of his house. Dodge rode so fast he beat us. He holds open the door for me to climb out. I wince once, and he's got me in his arms again.

"I really wish you'd put me down. My feet ain't broken."

"Quit your grumbling," he stammers with a country twang.

"The country boy does still live inside you," I tease.

He ignores me, marching up the steps, and carries me through the door Daddy has kicked open with the toe of his boot. "Put her on the couch," he orders.

Momma comes rushing over. "Let me take a look at you." She starts to undress me then looks around. "You boys need to step outside," she says to Daddy, Tucker, and Dodge.

When the door shuts behind them, Momma and Missy ease off my shirt. "You know it ain't like they ain't seen titties before." I giggle then regret it when pain shoots through my side.

"I don't think your daddy would like them boys seeing yours," Momma says. "Can you support her arm so I can take a look at her side?" She directs Missy.

With my arm braced by Missy, Momma lightly places her fingers on my side. "You've got some bruising under your arm and over your chest. Is this where it hurts when you take a deep breath in?"

"Yes," I whine.

"Gently lower her arm," she tells Missy. As soon as she does, Momma is standing over me, feeling my shoulder. "I think it may be dislocated rather than broken." She runs her hand toward my neck. "Your collarbone is definitely broken."

"It's good my shoulder ain't, though, right?"

"You need X-rays to make sure. But yes, better dislocated than broken. I'll get my bag and drive you to the hospital."

"You have your hands tied with River. Daddy can take me."

"Tucker and I will do it," Missy chimes in.

"No, you and Tucker spend time with family. I'm

sure I'll be in and out in no time. Besides, I have to get back to the vineyard for tonight's show."

Daddy barges back through the door with the other men. "Are you done yet?" he growls.

"She needs to go to the emergency room to get pictures of her shoulder. I don't believe it's broken, but her collarbone is for sure," Momma tells him.

"I can take her," Dodge volunteers.

"Like hell you will. She's my daughter. I'll take care of her." Daddy helps me off the couch.

Dodge purses his lips but doesn't dare argue with him. "I can go help set up at the vineyard. I'm sure you've left detailed instructions as to where everything goes."

"I did. They're on my computer. The password is in the register." I almost instantly regret telling him. My plans for the vineyard and all the sales are on my computer. I'm not sure I can trust him. "You know what, never mind, I'm sure I'll be back in time to take care of things."

He walks over to me. "You can trust me, Rose. I only want to help."

His gaze dances with mine, and I can see the sincerity in them. "Alright," I relent. 'Thank you."

CHAPTER NINE

ETHAN

"*D*on't give it another thought. I'll grab Noah, and we'll head to the vineyard. Give Rose my love and tell her not to worry. And yes, I'll keep an eye on Dodge." I hang up the phone with Boone and quickly call Noah, telling him to meet me at the vineyard. Before I can even hang up the phone, Jane is beeping in. I tell Noah to head over, and I switch to my wife.

"Hey darling," I answer.

"Clem just told me what happened to Rose. I'm going to come lend a hand at the vineyard."

"I'm headed there now, so is Noah. Where is Mercy?"

"She's attached to my hip as always." She laughs. "She'll love gobbling up some blueberries."

"The last time she did, it took two days to scrub the purple off her hands and lips." I chuckle.

"Yes, but she was adorable."

"That she was." A smile covers my face, thinking about it.

"Oh, I meant to tell you, something strange happened this morning."

The hair on the back of my neck stands up. "What?"

"Someone keeps calling my phone. The first time, whoever it was hung up right away. I thought it was a wrong number. The next time I answered, there was a long silence. The third time the same thing, but the call came from a different number. I'm sure it's nothing, except it made me a little uneasy."

"Next time, don't answer a number you don't know. Let it go to voicemail."

"I can't do that. I have clients that call my cell phone to make reservations."

"You shouldn't be using your personal phone for that."

"I'm not always at The Magnolia. I have to take the calls."

"That stops now. I'll change your number. All calls can be rolled over to the bed-and-breakfast phone. They can leave a message." A knot forms in my stomach.

"I shouldn't have said anything. I'm sure it's nothing."

"Look, it's my job to protect you and Mercy. If something makes you uncomfortable, I want to know about it right away."

There's a long bit of silence before she speaks. "Has something happened I should know about? You're going a tad overboard."

"You know Rossi is still out there somewhere."

"You think it's him? Seems like he's moved on by now."

"I don't know, but I can't ever let my guard down where he's concerned."

"Alright, then change my number," she sounds scared.

"I didn't mean to frighten you. I'm sure it's nothing. Please don't worry. I'm just being overprotective."

"I love that you make me feel safe and that you're so protective of our daughter."

"That's my job."

"I do feel safe with you, Ethan, with every aspect of my life. I'll tell you every day if you need the reassurance."

She knows I felt guilty for not making her feel secure in the fact that she could talk to me. I'd never judge her for her feelings. "No need. I believe you, darling."

"Good. Your two girls will meet you at the vineyard" She hangs up.

"My two girls," I say. "I love the sound of that." I would die for both of them. They are my world.

I glance in the rearview mirror, and there is a black car with dark windows running up close behind me. I speed up, and so does the driver. Lightly tapping my brakes, I wait to see what the car will do. The driver zips around beside me and runs even with me for a few moments, then speeds by me. The tinted windows were too dark to see inside. There's no plate on the car. Punching the gas pedal, I follow it until he races off down the highway out of town.

Slamming on my brakes, I come to a complete stop and run my hands through my hair. "Surely I'm being paranoid. Probably some punk kid out with his daddy's car. Nevertheless, after I've turned around headed in the right direction, I call Mike and let him know what happened with the car and Jane's phone.

I try to shake off my fear before I pull up to

Rose's vineyard. Dodge is already inside, giving the staff a hand. He chuckles when he sees me. "Rose called in for backup, didn't she?"

"No, Boone did."

He turns the computer in my direction. "This is what she needs done. There are chairs in the storage area behind the cellar." He points to the layout on the screen.

"She's very detailed, isn't she?" The property is all drawn out with a list of where everything can be found.

"She's very professional, that's for sure."

"Smart girl."

A look of admiration covers his face. "She sure is."

I head off to the storage area and toss the chairs in the back of my truck. When I get back to the stage area for the band, Noah, Jane, and Mercy have arrived.

"Hey, babe." Jane kisses me. I pick up Mercy, who's holding on for dear life to her mother's hand.

"Daddy," she says, giving me a wet messy kiss.

"She's been a handful this morning. I'm hoping she can burn off some energy while we're here."

"Don't let her too far out of your sight." I put her back on the ground.

"Are you worried because of the phone calls?"

"No, but I let Mike know about it. He wants me to bring him your phone. I'll take it to him once I've bought you another one."

"Can you wipe the worry off your face? We're safe." She brushes her hand over my forehead. "You've got a deep indentation between your eyebrows when something's hard on your mind."

I exhale. "Alright, I'll lighten up if you promise to keep your eyes peeled for anything out of sorts."

"I promise," she kisses me again.

"Now, go see if you and Mercy can help get food ready." She turns, and I swat her in the ass. She yelps and grins over her shoulder.

For the next hour, Noah and I work on setting up the stage and chairs. Rose bought extra lights to be hung. Noah gets a ladder and strings them over the seating area while I check on the keg of beer she had delivered. Leave it to her to think of the cowboys wanting their beer rather than a bottle of wine. Hauling the crates of wine to the mock bar she purchased for outdoor parties, I see a handwritten sign. "The beer is not for sale. The cup is. In order to obtain a cup, you have to purchase a bottle of wine."

"She is a smart woman." Dodge's voice comes from behind me.

"She knows a cowboy can't pass up an ice-cold beer."

"Yeah, and the wine will make the womenfolk happy." He moseys up beside me.

"You know, Chet thinks you're up to no good when it comes to Rose."

"He's wrong. I like Rose a lot. I'm sticking around to spend some time with Tucker, and I have a little business on the side. When all's done, I'll leave Rose alone, but I'd like to stay friends with her."

I look him up and down. "Friends, huh?" I chuckle.

"I'm going to help her expand her business."

I move up close to him. "And what do you get out of the deal?"

"I'm not expecting anything. Rose is a good businesswoman. She's not going to let anyone take advantage of her."

"I'd hope not, 'cause you'd have to face Boone if you hurt her."

He swallows hard. "I ain't aiming to hurt her, and he's not someone I want to reckon with."

I grasp his shoulder when I move by him. "You're smarter than you look."

I go inside the cafe to see if there is anything I

can help with. Jane is just getting off the phone. "That was Boone. He's on his way with Rose."

"How is she?"

"He said Clem was right, a broken collarbone, and a dislocated shoulder which has been put back in place. He said her side is pretty beat up with a lot of bruising but not broken. They did a couple tests that aren't back yet, but he said Rose insisted on leaving."

"She's as stubborn as all the other Calhoun women." I laugh. My gaze sweeps the cafe. "Where's Mercy?"

Jane glances around. "She was just right here."

Panic fuels my blood, and I step around Jane, looking in the kitchen. "Mercy!" I holler.

"She couldn't have gone far," Jane says.

"I told you not to take your eyes off her," I growl, pushing open the walk-in freezer door to make sure she's not inside.

"Mercy," Jane says this time. She looks underneath the counters, and I make my way to the pantry door.

Relief washes over me when I see her sitting in a pile of flour she spilled over on the floor. "She's in here," I say loudly.

Jane pushes by me and scoops her in her arms. "Thank God she's okay."

A rush of anger fills me. "Next time when I tell you not to let her out of your sight…" before I finish, Jane spins in my direction.

"I don't need you to patronize me right now." Her eyes glisten with tears.

I move into the pantry, letting the door shut behind me. Wrapping my hand around the back of her neck, I draw her and Mercy into me. "You're right. I'm sorry. I'm just a little spooked."

"Something else happened, didn't it?" she whispers.

"I'll tell you about it later. Let's go out and let our little princess pick blueberries before it gets too dark." I hold open the door.

"Do you want to stick around to hear the band play? We haven't been out in a while."

"If that's what you want. I'll ask Noah to take Mercy home with him."

"I would like that. The thought of dancing with my husband under the night sky is a turn-on." She covers Mercy's ears.

"Then far be it for me to say no to my wife," I deepen my voice for effect, and I see her eyes dilate.

I take Mercy from her arms and grab Jane's hand,

leading them out into the vineyard. Placing Mercy on her feet, she immediately starts picking blueberries. I twirl Jane flush to my body, all while keeping one eye trained on our daughter. Jane steps on her tiptoes, kissing me sweetly.

"I really am sorry, I spoke to you the way I did," I say against her lips.

"All's forgiven, cowboy."

"You know I would give my life for the two of you."

"Yes, I do. I feel the same way. I wouldn't want to live without either of you."

I nip at her ear. "Have I told you what a good mother you are?"

"I don't mind hearing it. Sometimes I think I'm awful at it."

I lean back to look at her face. "Why would you think that?"

She bites at her lower lip. "Because of the way I left the two of you."

"Like you said moments ago, all is forgiven. Mercy will never recall you not being in her life. She adores you, and so does this simple man."

"We've had this discussion before. There is nothing simple about you. You have many layers, Mr. York."

"That may be true, but I simply love you. No strings and unconditionally."

"You've proven that to me over and over. I don't deserve a man like you, but I'm thankful for you every day of my life, and Mercy couldn't ask for a better father."

"Quit saying you don't deserve me. There is nothing wrong with you, Jane. You're not broken anymore."

"Thanks to you and the way you love me." She kisses me again, but this time deepens our connection.

CHAPTER TEN

DODGE

*B*oone's big diesel parks out front of the vineyard next to the cafe. Patrons are already starting to show up. I run and open the door for Rose to get out. Her right arm is in a sling that is attached to a strap around her waist. Her hair is a mess, and she has a smear of dirt across her cheek. Holding out my hand, she takes it and gingerly climbs out, wincing.

"You should go straight to bed and let us handle the band tonight."

She yanks her hand from mine. "No way am I leaving this shindig to anyone. This is my responsibility. I'll be fine after a hot shower."

"I tried telling her the same thing, but she ain't

having it," Boone snarls, coming from around the driver's side.

"Okay, if you're determined to not rest, let me help you to your place so you can shower."

"I can help my daughter," Boone growls.

Before I can respond, Ethan has yelled Boone's name and is waving him over. "I'm more than capable of helping her, sir," I say.

"It's alright, Daddy. I'll be down in no time." She shoos him off.

Rose moves slowly, and I walk behind her, not sure of how to get to her space. "We'll go through the back, so I don't have to field a thousand questions." We walk through the backdoor of the cafe and up a flight of stairs. She opens the door, and I stand in the doorway, peering inside.

"Wow, this place is nice." It's larger than I imagined. It's decorated in a classy Farm-style look. Bright white on the walls, with brown raw wood beams on the ceiling. Several beaded chandeliers are hanging. Soft hues of blues and brown cover the oversized off-white couch, and beads hang from the curtains. It's all one big open room. The kitchen on one end, the bedroom on the other. The shower is in the corner by the bedroom with a clear glass shielding one side.

"Are you coming in?" Rose kicks off her shoes. "I could use help getting out of these chaps."

"You want me to help you, or do you want me to get Missy?"

"It's not like you haven't seen me naked before. At least partially." She moves in front of her bed. "Now, give me a hand."

Walking in, I shut the door behind me. Moving to her, I help her out of her chaps, then the sling. "Careful," I say, holding her arm in place as she tries to wiggle out of her pants. "Stop. Let me do it." I untie her red plaid shirt that's tied around her waist and carefully finagle her arm out. Then I unbutton her pants sliding them down her legs. I can't help but get hard. She's got the longest sexiest legs I've ever seen. My jaw flexes to keep from kissing her.

She takes her clothes from me and tosses them on the bed. "Could you fix me a glass of wine while I clean up?" She reaches into the shower and turns the water on.

I shuffle across the room to her kitchen, open the fridge, grab a bottle of wine and pour her a glass. The glass door of the shower steams up, and I can see her silhouette through it.

"Can you help me wash my hair?" she calls out.

I swallow hard. Don't touch her, I say to myself.

Placing the wineglass on the counter, I move toward her, rolling up my sleeves. When I'm in front of her, I try not to stare.

"Don't be shy now. I need your help." She hands me the bottle of shampoo. I pump it into my hand, and she turns her back to me. I can't take my gaze off the water dripping down her back to the crack of her ass. Damn, she's gorgeous.

She glances over her shoulder. "What are you doing back there?"

"Nothing," I groan. I spread the shampoo in my hands and start scrubbing her hair. I've never in my life taken care of a woman. I've had hot sex, but never have I ever bathed anyone. It's more erotic than I ever thought it would be. It feels good. Would I feel like this with any other woman other than Rose? What is it about her? I felt it all those years ago I met her. "Turn around," I say huskily.

She does. She peeks from one eye but doesn't say anything. She just watches me.

I scrub the top of her head then move her to rinse it out under the spray of the shower. I reach back, grabbing a towel. Once her hair is free of shampoo, she opens her eyes.

"I need to put conditioner in it, or this thick mane will tangle." She hands me another bottle.

"You're killing me," I groan.

"Please," she begs.

She steps back over to me and turns again. My jaw twitches, still trying to convince myself to keep this friendly. I repeat the process of lathering her hair. She rinses, and the towel comes out again. I gently wrap one in her hair and grab another, drying her gently.

"Thank you," she says. She moves to her closet and tosses out a pretty flowered dress and a pair of cowboy boots. "There is no way I can put these on by myself. Would you go ask Missy to help me?"

"I can do it."

"You've helped me enough, and I appreciate it, but I'd like Missy to do the rest. She'll be able to help me fix my hair, too."

"Alright." I reluctantly head downstairs. Was she testing me? She lets me shower her naked but doesn't want me to help her get her clothes on. Or, did she not trust herself any further with me? Stomping around to the front of the cafe, I find Missy clinging to Tucker's arm.

"How is she?" she asks when she sees me.

"She asked me to come get you to you help her with her clothes and hair."

"Okay," she states, running off.

"How come you're all wet?" Tucker points at the front of my shirt.

"I, um...I had to turn the shower on for Rose. I misjudged the spray of the water."

"You helped her shower?" He chuckles. "But come get Missy for the rest?"

"I only did what she asked me to do," I mumble.

"I love you, brother, but please don't get involved with Rose. She's way too good for you."

"Ouch!"

"You know what I mean. You like playing the field and have no intention of sticking around Salt Lick. Rose has her act together, and her life is here. I just don't want you to hurt her, that's all."

"So, it's okay if she breaks my heart?"

He stares at me for a moment. "Are you for real? You have honest feelings for Rose?"

"Of course not." I half chuckle, hiding any emotion I might have toward her. "You're right. She's too good for the likes of me. I enjoy my life the way it is. No need to complicate things."

"Good. I'm glad we're on the same page." He clasps my shoulder.

We mingle in the crowd and taste test a few bottles of wine. I'm more of a beer man, but I have to admit, I really like the flavors Rose has created. We help Boone and Ethan with bringing out a few more chairs. The place is packed, and the band starts playing.

Out of the corner of my eye, I see Rose and Missy in the crowd. She's beautiful and elegant, yet at the same time ordinary. I press the wineglass to my lips and watch her mingle. Her eyes light up when she talks to people. She draws them in like flies to honey. Natural beauty flows through her every move. I've never met another woman like her. She's honest, and in my line of work, that's hard to find. Her southern drawl is even sexy. I love that's she's not afraid to share her true self with others.

My phone vibrates in my pocket, drawing me out of my thoughts. "Excuse me, I have to take this." I hold the phone up to Tucker. I wait to answer it until the sound of the band is muted by me walking away toward the parking area.

"Why are you calling me on a Saturday night?" I ask my boss, answering the phone.

"I've got a buyer in Northern California who is very interested in purchasing the vineyard. He said he's willing to pay double whatever it's worth."

"I haven't worked up a true value on it. I know what it's worth at the moment, but her taking it international will more than likely triple the value."

"All you need to worry about is convincing her to sell and be quick about it."

"I've already told you it's going to take some time."

"Use that pretty boy charm on her. It's worked in the past."

"Rose is different. She's not like any other client we've ever had."

"It should be simple. She's a southern bell. You can outsmart her."

"I think you've misjudged her completely. She's very smart and focused."

"You aren't falling for this girl, are you? I'd hate to think my highest-paid employee would risk losing his career over a ranch hand's daughter."

My jaw flexes, holding in my anger. He has no idea what hard work it is growing up on a ranch. Rose wasn't handed anything. She worked hard with the support of her family and has been very successful in a short amount of time. I admire her. "These are good people, not like the ones you work with. I need time."

"The clock is ticking," he says.

"You may have to move the hands back. I'll be in touch." I hang up. Walking back into the band area.

Missy is being coerced to go on stage. When Rose sees me, she heads in my direction.

"I knew we'd convince her to sing." She's all smiles. We stand next to Tucker and face the stage. Rose looks at me a little sideways. "You alright?"

"Yeah, why?" I frown.

"You have a worry line on your forehead."

"Nothing for you to worry about." I'm such a liar. It's me she needs to be concerned with stealing her company.

As she stands between my brother and me and Missy sings, I find myself wanting to hold Rose's hand. What's wrong with me? I don't hold hands, yet my pinky finger seems to have a mind of its own as I loop mine with hers. She looks at me and grins, then folds her hand with mine. It's the sweetest thing I've ever felt.

The crowd goes crazy for Missy. "She really is good." Tucker beams.

"She should be doing this for a living," I respond.

"Missy decided she didn't want that kind of life. She's happy as a lamb being married, racing horses, and now a new baby on the way. She wouldn't have it any other way," Rose states.

"She's a much better person than me. I don't

know that I could sacrifice what I want out of life for another person."

"That's why you have no business ever getting married." Tucker laughs.

I release Rose's hand. He's right. I'm here for a purpose, and I can't let anything sway me differently.

***

THE CROWD of people starts thinning out as soon as the band ends its last song. It's after midnight when the final person leaves.

"We'll come back tomorrow and help clean up," Boone says, kissing Rose's forehead. "You look exhausted. You should get some sleep."

"Thanks for helping me today," she tells him.

"That's what family is for. I'll see you in the morning." He walks toward his truck.

"We're going to head out too," Missy says, rubbing her belly.

"You were fantastic," Rose says with a hug.

"We'll come in the morning and help too," Tucker adds. "What about you, Dodge? You headed to the Magnolia?"

"Yeah, I'll help Rose to her flat, and then I'll leave."

"I can do that," Missy states.

"Don't be silly. You go home and get some sleep. Ain't any reason Dodge can't help me." Rose shoos them off.

"You do know I can manage the stairs with one hand," Rose states, flippantly over her shoulder.

"I know, you're one independent woman. I just want to make sure you don't need anything before I leave."

She opens the door to her place. "You could stay the night. We're both grown adults, capable of sharing a bed."

"As sweet as that sounds, you know that's not true. I don't think I could sleep next to you and not want to have you."

Her eyes darken. "Normally, I wouldn't mind, but my shoulder is throbbing. All I want to do is take a pain pill and fall into bed."

"Let me help you change, and I'll leave."

"See, you can be a gentleman." She giggles.

In my head, there is nothing gentlemanly I want to do with her. Tucker's right. I have to keep limits between us. She is too good for me.

She pulls out a pair of pajamas, and I help her change, settling her into bed. "Good night, Rose."

"You sure you don't want to stay?" she asks with a yawn and her eyes nearly closing.

"I'll see you tomorrow."

CHAPTER ELEVEN

ROSE

I wake to my arm aching and wince as I roll to my side. For a moment, I forget Dodge didn't stay the night. Part of me really wanted him to. I like him more than I care to admit. He was such a gentleman to help me shower last night. I was testing him. I get the idea he thinks he's not such a good guy, but deep down, I know he is, at least I hope so. He intrigues me trying to play city boy when I know a cowboy is just under the surface. He looks too damn good in his blue jeans and Stetson not to be.

I sit on the edge of the bed when I hear Missy calling me from the other side of the door. "I'm coming." Dang, my body hurts. It will teach me to leave the horse riding to other members of my family.

She knocks again.

"It ain't locked," I holler.

"You don't lock your door at night?" Missy scolds coming inside.

"It's a habit from living on the ranch." I stand.

"Yeah, but you live way out here by yourself." She brushes my hair from my shoulder and looks around.

"Dodge didn't stay the night," I snort.

"Oh, I…"

"Don't worry. The city boy ain't my type."

"You know, he's not as bad as everyone makes him seem. He has a really sweet side."

"His own brother doesn't even defend him," I snicker as I walk into the bathroom to pee. "Why are you here so early?"

"Tucker and Boone wanted to come early, so you didn't stress about the mess outside. I thought I'd lend a hand in the cafe." She walks into the bathroom and puts toothpaste on my toothbrush, handing it to me.

"It's only open a few hours on Sunday, but I'd sure appreciate the help."

"I'll help you get dressed, then I'll make us a cup

of coffee."

"I can dress myself." I spit in the sink and wipe my mouth. "Just help me get out of this sling."

"Are you supposed to take it off so soon?"

"When have I ever done as I've been told," I snort. "Besides, I need to move it."

She helps me take it off but insists on helping me clothe myself. I have to admit, it still hurts a lot and her putting on my shoes was a lifesaver.

"Do you want me to braid your hair, so it's out of the way?" She holds up a brush.

"That's a good idea." I sit, and she runs the brush through my thick red hair before she braids it, fastening it at the bottom.

"There, all done."

"Thanks, Missy."

"How about that coffee so we can catch up?"

I follow her down the stairs to the cafe and show her where everything is located. "I'll take out some muffins and warm them while you brew the coffee." My arm feels a little better without the sling, but I'm sure to move it slowly. After zapping the muffins, I take a seat at the cafe bar top, and Missy pours the hot cup of Joe.

"You were amazing last night. Do you ever regret giving up a chance at having a career singing?"

"Not for one moment. My life is perfect." Her eyes gleam with love.

"That's what I told Dodge last night."

"I take it you ain't still mad at him." She sits next to me.

"Actually, he's going to be helping me grow internationally."

"So you're using him?" She giggles.

Am I? I know that was my first thought. "I'll be paying him for his knowledge."

She squints at me. "You two done did the dirty, didn't you?"

I choke on my coffee. "Why would you think such a thing?"

"Because your cheeks turned pink when you talked about him."

"That don't mean nothing." I try to brush her off.

"Don't lie to me. I see it written all over your face." She points at me.

"Fine, we had a quickie in the cellar. It's out of my system, and it won't happen again." I straighten my spine as if I have any dignity.

"When I suggested you get laid, it wasn't meant to be Dodge." She leans over, whispering even though it's just the two of us in the cafe.

"Better him than a complete stranger," I shrug.

"I'm not so sure about that. You know he's always liked you."

"We're both grown adults with very different lives. We can have a no strings attached agreement."

"I thought you said it wasn't going to happen again."

"It's not...I just meant...if Dodge and I..."

"If you and Dodge what?" Daddy's voice blares from behind me.

Why do I feel like a small child again? "If Dodge and I worked together, we'd have to come to an agreement on what I'd pay him." I'm not a good liar, and Daddy will see right through me.

"Why would you have any need to work with Dodge? He buys and sells companies, and yours is not for sale." He walks behind the counter and pours a mug of coffee.

"Yeah, I don't think it's a good idea you have any business dealings with my brother." Tucker joins Missy at her side.

"You two need to let Rose handle her own business," Missy scolds them.

"Look, your brother has knowledge I need to take this place up a few notches. I'm more than willing to pay him for his time."

"Dodge doesn't do anything unless he can profit

from it," Tucker says.

"I don't think you give your brother enough credit. He's been very good to me."

"And, I think you're being a tad bit naive." Daddy slams his mug on the counter.

"Daddy!"

"Just saying, darling." He shrugs.

"Where is Dodge anyway?" Missy asks.

"He called me this morning and said he wouldn't make it out here today. He had work to get done."

That's odd. He was looking forward to spending the day with his brother. I check my phone to see if he called me. Nothing. I text him. *You okay? Tucker said you ain't coming to the* vineyard *today?*

Three dots appear immediately, followed by his response. *"I have work that needs to be done. We can meet tomorrow and discuss the future plans of the* vineyard."

Future plans? I type, *"The only plans we need to discuss is how to market internationally."*

"That's what I meant. I'll see you tomorrow."

Why such curt responses? I thought things were alright between us. The man held my hand, for Pete's sake. Who does that? Maybe his brother is right about him.

"Everything okay?" Missy runs her hand down

my arm.

"Yeah, yeah," I brush her off.

"We got all the chairs put away, and the mess cleaned up. Anything else you need us to do?" Tucker asks.

"No. I appreciate it."

"I'm taking Tucker shooting if you ladies don't need us," Boone states.

"That would be perfect. I'll stay here and help with the cafe. Maybe you two should invite Dodge to go too. You don't get to spend much time with him," Missy adds.

"I'll call him, but the man said he was busy." He steps outside.

"You don't mind, do you, Uncle Boone?" Missy smiles

"It's a little late for the ask, but no. It will give me a chance to get to know him better."

Tucker pops back in. "He said he'd meet us at the main house."

"I thought he was too busy?" I frown.

"He said he'd catch up this evening." Tucker lifts one shoulder.

Is he avoiding me? Perhaps I am naive. I'll have to keep our work on the up and up. No more googly eyes at city boy.

. . .

***

As I start to roll down the door of the cafe, I see Dodge's car coming down the long drive with the sun setting behind it. I walk out onto the deck, leaning one arm on the railing, waiting for him.

He gets out sportin' a black Stetson, and my heart leaps. "I thought you were with your brother," I say casually, not wanting him to know how glad I am to see him.

"I cut out early." His boots stomp on the wooden deck until he is next to me. "I wanted to spend time with the prettiest redhead in town." He grins.

"It's been a long day, Dodge, and my shoulder aches."

"Grab a bottle of wine and two glasses. I want to take you somewhere."

"We can drink here."

"I know we could, but I really want to take you out."

My energy level picks up a notch.

"Come on. I bought this new hat thinking you'd

like it. Not to mention how good I look in it." He drags it from his head, laying it over his heart.

I can't help but snicker at his arrogance. "Fine. I'll have to change. I can't have you looking prettier than me." I push off the railing, and he snags my hand before I can get away.

"You're perfect just the way you are. Do you trust me, Rose?"

I cross my arms over my chest. "That's a loaded question."

"Fair enough. Trust me just for tonight." He holds out his hand for me to take.

"I have to close the cafe first."

He walks past me through the open door, snags a bottle of wine and glasses, then comes back out and, with one hand, rolls the door closed. "Anything else?" he asks.

"That covers it."

"Then get your pretty little ass in my car."

"What happened to keeping this platonic?" I giggle, following him.

"Tonight is whatever you want it to be. I just want us to have fun together and show you a different side of me."

I hope it's not a side I fall madly in love with. "The city boy has another side?" I tease.

He zooms down the drive. "There are all sorts of things you don't know about me, Rose Methany." He has a devilish look in the speckled colors of his eyes that make my lady parts ache.

"Where are you taking me anyways?"

"Rest back and take a nap. It's a bit of a drive, but it'll be worth it."

I adjust the back of my seat, curling to my side, tucking my hands under my cheek. "I'm going to take you up on that nap. Wake me when we get there."

***

"DAMN, GIRL. YOU SNORE," Dodge says as he lightly shakes me awake.

Sitting up quickly, I pull down the shade, and the mirror on it lights up. I wipe my eyes and try to fix my messy braid.

"You look gorgeous." He chuckles.

"I don't snore." I scrunch my nose at him. Closing the visor, I see the bright neon lights on the building. "You brought me to the Bucking Broncho?" I squeal.

"Margret gave me a brochure on this place. She

assured me you'd like it."

I've been wanting to come here to watch the bull riders and maybe bring one home. I probably shouldn't share that thought with him. "It looks like so much fun," I say instead.

He takes my hand in his as we make it to the entrance. The inside is jam-packed full of people. We manage to snag a small table as a couple leaves. The back of the bar is a lite up stage where the bucking bull rocks back and forth, slinging off its victims. In the middle is a dance floor with a live band off to the side.

Dodge holds up two fingers and mouths beer to the waitress who passes by us. "Well, what do you think so far?" he asks, grinning from ear to ear.

"I think I'd like it better if you'd dance with me."

"I don't dance much," he says.

"All you have to do is sway that ass of yours. Besides, I can't dance my best with a bum shoulder." The waitress drops off two bottles of beer as she sweeps by our table.

Dodge presses the cold bottle to his lips. "I'll pass."

I stand abruptly. "Fine. I'm sure I can find some cowboy who wants to rock his hips with mine." I glance around the bar only to find Dodge in my face.

"Not tonight, you're not." He grips my elbow and walks me out to the dance floor.

My body moves to the music, and I dance around him as he stands still, biting his bottom lip as he watches me. Turning my back to him, I move with the music against him. His hands find my hips, and I feel him start to move. It's sensual and sexy. He skirts me around to face him, and it's me that stands stock-still drooling over him. "I thought you said you couldn't dance." I literally have drool at the corner of my mouth.

"I said, I don't dance much. I never said I couldn't dance." He sports a smile as he grabs my hips, shuffling me around the dance floor. When the band changes songs, a line dance forms, and I fully expect Dodge to drag me off the dance floor. Instead, I find myself next to him, with him knowing every step. He moves with such ease and sexiness. I hear a couple of women behind him giggling, talking about how hot he is. He's right; this is a side of him I haven't seen. My favorite part so far.

When the song ends, we head back to our table. "Where'd the city boy learn to line dance?" I ask, out of breath.

"You forget, I didn't always live in the city. Truth be told, there is one country bar in the city where I live in California. Every now and then, when I was alone, I'd slink off to the bar and dance all night."

"You're full of surprises." I clink my beer bottle with his. "And here I thought you were all business all the time."

"I get out of my suit on occasion."

"I like this occasion." In fact, I'm loving everything about him at this moment.

As the music dies down, the microphone cracks over the speaker. "The next bull rider is originally from Lexington, Kentucky. He comes here tonight all the way from California to take on our bull. Give a hand to Dodge Anderson." The crowd goes crazy.

My eyes light up. "What? How?"

"I called ahead and set up a time."

"How'd you know I'd come with you?"

"I didn't, but you're here." He smiles.

I follow him to the back of the bar. He signs a paper on a clipboard and listens to the rules.

"Have you done this before?" I say loudly over the crowd of people.

He inches close to me, speaking into my ear. "Why? You worried I might injure my most valuable part?" He immediately steps back and toward the bull.

I want to scream, yes, I'm worried, but instead,

my gaze is glued to him. He hikes a leg over the bull, straddling him, and the leather on the saddle creaks along with my heart. At this very moment in time, I'm so in love with him. The aching in my body is overwhelming. It's like fireworks shooting off.

Dodge holds on tight with one hand, and his right arm goes in the air above his head. His thigh muscles tighten, getting a better grip. He nods slightly, indicating he's ready. The bull starts its rocking until it's on full-on bucking mode. The crowd is cheering, and I'm holding my breath. Dodge's gaze cuts in my direction and doesn't let go. His look is powerful and says so much to me. I know I've sworn off having sex with him, but what I'd give for him to be riding me right now like he's riding that bull. For the first time in my life, I want it to be more than just sex. I want the emotion he's glaring into me right now. The depth of what he's feeling is raw and demanding.

When the bull stops, I let out the breath I'd been holding, but not the emotions. Dodge climbs off the bull, and several women run over to him, swooning like groupies. Their hands are all over his chest, touching him. I don't like it one bit, and neither does Dodge. He brushes them off and heads directly toward me like a man on a mission.

"Let's dance," is all he says.

We spend the next hour on the dance floor enjoying each other's company. I find myself in uncharted territory as I feel jealous, which is a new experience for me at the looks he's getting from other women. When the band announces its final song, Dodge takes me by the hand, walking me out. He drapes his arm around me with his hand landing at my hip as we make our way to his car.

"Did you have fun?" he asks, opening my door.

I answer him with a kiss. "Yes, thank you."

His eyes darken, and his voice is raspy. "Believe me when I tell you it was my pleasure."

He just set the hook. I've fallen for him, hook, line, and sinker, as my daddy would say. "I think most of it was mine."

He glances between us at the bulge in his jeans. "I think I could argue the point."

I drape my arms around his neck and look out into the night sky. "You wouldn't happen to have a blanket in the back seat of your car?"

"I do." His jaw tightens.

"Then get your sweet ass in the car. I have the perfect place for us to go."

As we drive back toward Salt Lick, we flirt and laugh with one another. I really love this side of him, and I'm not ready for it to end. "Take a right." I point down a dirt road.

"Where the hell are you taking me, woman?" He makes the bumpy turn up a hill.

"You'll see. Keep going until you can't drive any further."

We climb the hill until we hit the top. I jump out, pull the blanket out of the back seat, and spread it out on the ground. Flipping off my shoes, I lay flat on the blanket. Dodge removes his boots and joins me.

"You can see the stars for miles," I say.

He rests his hands behind his head with his elbows out. "This isn't where I thought we'd end up with the vibes you were giving me at the bar."

I roll to my side. "This is exactly where I want to be with you."

"It is beautiful," he admits.

I lie back.

"What is it you want from me, Rose?"

"Right here, in this moment." I take his hand in mine. "I want to spend hours talking, getting to really know you. The real you. Not the man that hides behind the business suit. The one I saw tonight. Tell me everything about him."

His hand squeezes mine. "I can do that."

CHAPTER TWELVE

ETHAN

"Any luck tracing the phone number on Jane's cell?"

"No, I'm afraid not," Mike says.

"What about the vehicle that was following me?"

"We don't have a plate to track it, only a description of the car, and there's been no sight of it in Salt Lick."

"I appreciate you looking. Let me know if anything develops." I hang up.

"What are you doing here on a Sunday afternoon?" Tally walks into my office.

"I could ask you the same thing?" I lean back in my chair.

"I left my notes here, and I need to review them

for a meeting I have tomorrow." She sits. "You didn't answer my question."

"Jane's been receiving some odd phone calls, and Mike was trying to trace them for me."

"And, you didn't want Jane upset."

"Right. It may be nothing."

"Sounds like something to me if you're concerned. You think it's Rossi?"

"My gut tells me it is."

"How would he have gotten Jane's personal number?"

"Good question." I tap a finger to my bottom lip.

"Maybe he's planted someone on the inside. Any new men on the ranch?"

"There's always extra hands this time of year, but Boone vets every one of them."

"I hope you figure it out." She stands. "Let me know if I can do anything to help."

"I will. Thanks, Tally."

She walks to the doorway then stops, looking over her shoulder. "Be careful, Ethan."

She looks as if she wants to say something else but instead marches out. I glance at my watch and realize I'm supposed to meet my hot little wife for lunch at Nita's place. I tuck her new phone in my pocket and lock the door behind me. She's sitting in a booth at the back of the diner with Chet.

She slides in when she sees me. "Hey, babe."

"I didn't know you were coming too." I shake Chet's hand.

"Your mother needed to do inventory at her shop. I kept trying to help her, but she said I was in her way, so I thought I'd have some pie."

"If my mother asks, I didn't see a thing." I chuckle.

"Smart man. I knew I always liked you." He scoops pie and ice cream in his mouth.

"I was telling Daddy about the phone calls. Was Mike able to find out anything?"

"No, but you shouldn't have any more problems." I dig the new phone out of my pocket and hand it to her. "Don't give out your number for work purposes."

"I hope you put a tracker in this one," Chet says, between bites.

"I did."

"I don't know that I like you keeping tabs on me all the time," Jane huffs.

"You doing something you shouldn't be?" Chet grunts.

She rolls her eyes at him like a teenager.

"It's for your own protection," I tell her. "And Mercy's."

"I know you're right, but it feels like an invasion into my privacy."

"I think she protests too much." Chet winks at me when she's not looking.

"Daddy!"

He snorts. "I'm only giving you a hard time. I want you and Mercy safe as much as Ethan does."

"You keep teasing me, and I'm going to tell Winnie about that pie you're scarfing down."

His fork stops just short of his mouth. "You wouldn't."

"Keep it up and watch me." This time she winks at me.

"Damn Calhoun women trying to ruin any pleasure a man my age has left," he grumbles.

Jane reaches over the table, covering his hand with hers. "You know it's because we all love you and want you to be around for many more years to come."

"I'm too mean and ornery to be cutting out anytime soon, so quiet your worrying."

She sits back, laughing. "If meanness keeps you alive, then you're going to outlive us all."

"You watch your tongue, young lady." He jabs his fork at her, and she laughs harder.

The waitress comes over and takes our order. Jane gives her the menu then looks out the window. "Hey, isn't that Tally?" She points across the street.

She's wearing a pair of shades talking to someone who has a hat covering his eyes. "Yes, it is."

"Did she finally get her own man?" she snickers.

"She didn't mention it."

"He doesn't look like he's from around these parts," Chet states.

"How can you tell. You can't see his face," Jane asks.

"His shoes are too fancy, and I don't know anyone in Salt Lick who wears a college ring. A ring in these parts could cost you a hand if it gets caught in a piece of equipment."

"He's right," I say.

"You two are being overly cautious. So what? She's talking to a man from out of town. Tally knows a lot of people. Besides, as long as it's not a Calhoun, why do you care?"

"I don't care who she is dating, but I do care about strangers in Salt Lick."

"Good thing you don't work at the Magnolia Mill. You'd be checking out all our customers."

"You're right. I'm sorry." I squeeze her thigh.

"Besides, you have nothing to worry about with my new handy dandy tracker in my phone." She holds it in the air with a smirk covering her face.

"Promise me you'll keep it on you."

She places a quick kiss to my lips. "If it makes you feel better, I promise."

"Good lord, if Winnie tried to put a tracker in my phone, I'd lose my shit," Chet bemoans.

"How do you know she hasn't?" Jane says, crossing her arms over her chest.

"She wouldn't," he states, then stares at his cell phone.

"She needs one that tracks what you eat and smoke in a given day," she taunts him.

"I've had about enough of your nonsense for one day." He tosses his napkin and some cash on the table then scoots out of the booth.

"Oh, Daddy, I was only kidding," she snorts.

"Don't matter none. I've got other places I can be where people respect me," he grumbles.

"Where would that be?" Jane leans in and whispers just loud enough for him to cut his scowl at her.

"I'll see you later at the house, don't bring my daughter with you," he says, then scuffs off through the diner.

"You're the only person I know that can aggravate the shit out of that man, and he still adores you." I tug at a strand of her long blond hair.

"I love messing with him. But, he really does need to cut down on the sweets and red meat."

"Chet would sooner lob off his right arm than not eat red meat. He's a cattleman, for goodness sakes."

Our food comes, and we enjoy a meal together, flirting with one another. As soon as we're done, Jane glances at her watch. "I have to go pick up Mercy from Ellie's. She took all the kids down by the river and wanted Mercy to join them."

"I forgot to ask Boone how River was doing?"

"Clem says she thinks he's a little better today."

"Good. I know he was really worried about him."

"I'm going to run some chicken and dumplings over. It's River's favorite."

"Why don't I meet you back at the house, and we can have some alone time while Mercy naps."

"Sounds good to me. Give me about an hour."

I kiss her before I shut her door and watch her back out onto the road that runs through the middle of town. As I walk down the block to my car, my phone vibrates. There's a photo text from Jane. I open it, and she's sent me a picture of her bare breasts. I click on the phone icon and call her.

"Aren't you driving?" My voice is husky even to me.

"I just wanted you to have a little glimpse of what you'll be getting later." She giggles.

"You shouldn't be driving and taking pictures. It ain't safe."

"Lord, you sound like my daddy. Just enjoy the snapshot," she snorts.

"I didn't say I didn't enjoy it, but I think I'll have to come up with some punishment for you later."

"That's the man I love! I'll be waiting for you at home." She hangs up.

"Damn, woman," I grumble, adjusting my crotch before I climb behind the wheel.

As I head out of town, I see the man Tally was talking to sitting in his dark grey Jeep. His sunglasses are still in place, and he's talking to someone on his phone. His head turns in my direction as I pass him. Taking a quick glance at his license plate, I memorize it and call Mike to research it. I don't know why he makes me feel uneasy, but he does. When I'm stopped at a red light, I call Tally.

"It's Sunday, Ethan. Whatever it is can wait," she answers.

"Who was the guy you were talking to across from the diner?"

"What guy?"

"The one in the Jeep."

"Oh, he was just someone asking directions." Her voice rises a notch or two.

"Directions to where, Tally?"

"He was looking for a place to stay for a few days. I directed him to the lodge at the end of town."

"What business did he have in town?"

"I don't know, Ethan. I didn't grill him. It's no big deal. People pass through Salt Lick all the time."

I feel as if she's hiding something by the way her tone is wavering. "Let me know if you see him again in town." I disconnect before she can answer. Instead of heading home to my wife, I make a U-turn to Mike's office. He waves me into his office when he sees me through the glass barrier.

"What did you find out?" I say, grabbing my Stetson from my head, and laying it on his desk.

"You didn't give me much time. Why are you so worked up?"

"Did you find out anything or not?" I growl.

Mike holds his hand in the air. "You need to calm down. Nothing so far has led to Rossi. I think you're jumping the gun here."

I blow out a long breath, running my hand through my hair. "I can't help the gut feeling I have about all of this."

"The tag is registered to a Brian Long from Nevada." He turns his computer toward me so I can see his picture on the screen.

"That's not the same man that was inside of it."

"So you got a good look at him?"

"He had on dark glasses and a hat, but his hair was dark, not blond."

He punches in a few numbers and picks up the phone. His fingers tap on the desk as it rings several times. He covers the receiver with his hand. "It's going to voicemail," he says, then leaves a message for him to call back.

"You'll let me know the minute you hear from him." I stand, grasping my hat.

"I'll give him until tomorrow to call back."

"And, if he doesn't?" I raise a brow.

"Then I'll make some more phone calls. In the meantime, try to relax and not scare the hell out of your wife until we know something."

"Can you put a man on Tally?"

"The mayor? You think she has something to do with this? You're stretching it, brother. You forget, he almost killed her too in the fire."

He's right; I'm sure I'm being paranoid. Her meeting him was probably innocent, like she claims. "Thanks for the help, man."

"*W*hat the hell?" I shove my truck into park and swing open the door.

"Please don't get all fired up," Winnie hollers, climbing out and trying to keep up with me.

Boone has a man by the collar shoved against the side of my house. "I don't know who the hell you are, but you're trespassing." Spit splatters in the man's face as Boone snarls. "Evidently, you aren't capable of reading the signs posted on the property!"

"I'm here on business with the owner," he chokes out.

"That would be me, and I don't recall having any business with you," I say, walking up behind Boone.

"He was snooping in the window and scared the

hell out of my wife and son," Boone seethes, tightening his grip.

"You should get the hell off my property before he chokes the life out of you," I say. Walking over to the porch, I pick up my shotgun then move to the bottom step. "You can let him go now," I nudge my head toward the man whose face is turning red.

Boone drops him to his feet, and I aim at him.

The guy lifts his hands in the air. "I ain't armed, mister. I'm sorry. I only wanted to check out the property. I spoke with Molly a few days ago and made an offer on this place. You turned it down."

I raise the shotgun to get a better aim. "I ain't selling, and you're trespassing like the man said."

"I'll double my offer," he hollers.

I rest the shotgun to the ground. "Why? The first offer was more than I could ever spend."

"This is the best piece of land in all of Kentucky, and developers are dying to get their hands on it."

"Death is what will happen to you if you step foot on this property again." Boone looms over him.

He skates out of Boone's reach. "Just think about it. I can have a written offer to you within twenty-four hours." He runs to his car and skids out.

Placing the shotgun down, I walk inside with Winnie. Clem was watching out of the window.

"You aren't going to consider his offer, are you?" Clem says, stepping over to me.

"Maybe I should. This place is nothing but hard work for the rest of my family's lives. It's been a fight all these years to keep this land." I sit in my recliner. "I'm too old to battle anymore."

Clem sits on the floor in front of me with River in her lap. "This ranch, our land, is part of our family. There is no other place in this world I want my son to grow up. We're all in this together, Daddy. It's our fight now. It's a fight I'm willing to endure for your grandchildren to inherit one day. There is no better education they can get from what they can learn from this place. You've taught us all hard work, love of family, and how to live off the land. These are things I want to teach my son. No amount of money can buy him what this place is worth to each of us. We've all prospered from what you've built here. Yes, there will be years we struggle, but it's well worth it."

"I want my family to have an easier life than I've had." I sigh.

"Nothing worth having is easy. We earn our ways as it should be." Boone steps behind Clem in a show of support.

"If it's money you want, Daddy, we'll give you every penny we have," Clem says.

"Pish, money don't mean nothing to me."

Clem places her hand on mine. "Then don't consider selling. We got this, all of us."

"She's right, Chet," Boone backs her up.

"You'd never forgive yourself if you sold this land." Winnie steps up beside me. "This is your legacy for your family. For River." She points at him.

"Come here, boy." River jumps in my lap. "You feeling better, son?"

He nods.

"All his tests came back normal. I can't tell you how relieved I was."

Boone places his hand on Clem's shoulder. "We were."

"I was so afraid he had inherited my leukemia." She peers up at Boone.

"The boy is good. He's going to get sick like all kids do. You can't go in panic mode every time the boy gets a sniffle or a bellyache," I tell her. "I think you've been cooped up long enough. What do you say to a horseback ride with your grandpa?" I ruffle his hair.

"I don't know, Daddy."

"Let him go," Boone interjects. "It will be good for him to have some fresh air."

"Alright. Just don't be gone too lone."

River climbs down, and I stand. As I do, a heaviness fills my chest for a moment. I stretch, trying to play it off.

"You alright?" Winnie asks.

"I'm fine. You worry too darn much." She keeps an eagle eye on me as I take River's hand and lead him out to the barn.

He stands by my side as I saddle my horse. "You ready?"

He nods his little head.

When I pick him up, the pressure in my chest returns with more intensity. My jaw flexes to steer back the discomfort as I take some deep breaths in.

"You okay, Grandpa?"

"Yes. I wouldn't let anything stop me from spending time with you." Putting my foot in the stirrup, I swing my leg over, sitting behind him. I take the reins, moving the horse out to the barn. My chest continues to ache. I'm not going to let it stop me. If I die on this horse with my grandson today, it will be the way I want to go, not locked up in a house eating vegetables from the garden.

"I want to see the fish." He points toward the river.

"You and I will have to go fishing one day soon, son." I steer the horse through the field down where the river widens. The bluegill catfish and stripped bass hang out in the deeper water.

Climbing down, I help the boy get off. He wades in the water, and I find a rock to prop up on, waiting for my chest to let up. I keep an eye on him, but quickly gaze up to the sky. It's a beautiful day to die, but today ain't my day to meet my maker. I dig into my jean jacket pocket and pull out an amber bottle containing my lifeline. I spill one nitro out and place it under my tongue, letting it melt and ease the pain.

"Is that candy, Grandpa?" His eyes light up.

"No, son, it's not." I laugh, pushing it deep into my pocket. "When we get back, I know where your grandma stashes the cookies."

"Momma said I can't have any until my tummy hasn't hurt for a couple of days." He frowns, looking at the ground.

"What your momma don't know won't hurt her. Come sit beside me." I motion him over, and he takes the rock next to me. "Your momma, when she was a little girl, ate a whole cake. Her mother had made her a birthday cake and put it in the fridge for her party the next day. She couldn't wait to eat it. When we all went to bed, she snuck downstairs and ate the entire chocolate cake."

"She did?" His eyes grow large. "Did her momma get mad?"

"When we got up the next morning, we found her on the floor. It looked like chocolate exploded everywhere. Your momma spent the night puking her guts up." I chuckle. "She swore she'd never eat cake again."

"But she did, didn't she?" He tilts his head.

"Yep. It wasn't six hours later she was digging into the store-bought cake her momma had to buy to replace the one she scarfed down like a sow."

He laughs. "She can't get mad at me for having a cookie."

"She can, but we ain't gonna tell her." I tweak his nose.

"You feeling all better now, Grandpa?"

"I am. Go try to catch me one of those fish."

He hops up and runs back to the water.

I sure do miss my kids being young. They were a pain in my ass at times, but I loved them. I've had the pleasure of watching all of them grow up. Wyatt turned out to be a fine man. In a million years, I never thought he'd be a rancher. Amelia was right about one thing—he is the smartest of the bunch. He's more like his momma than all of them. Ellie, well, Ellie is Ellie. God love her. She'd give you the shirt off her back, but if you cross her, she'd be the first to skin it off your body. She is her father's daughter. Bear is a kind soul unless you rile him. He's a better husband and father than I ever was. Even from a young age, Bear just wanted to be loved. He found the perfect spouse in Nita.

"I almost caught one, Grandpa," River yells.

"Keep trying."

Clementine was a handful as a young girl. I chuckle to myself. I guess that ain't changed much. Thank goodness she has Boone to keep her in line. She's my baby girl and always will be. As if that wasn't enough, I've been lucky enough to get to know Noah and Jane. I missed out on their childhood, but boy howdy am I glad I didn't miss the rest of their lives. Noah is a fine young man. I couldn't be prouder, and I can't take any credit. Winnie says he looks the most like me. Jane is a spitfire. A little broken at times. She reminds me a lot of Ellie. Tough on the outside, but soft on the inside. I didn't think much of Ethan when he first showed up on my doorstep with Clem all those years ago. He's turned into a great man. He loves hard and doesn't let go.

He has more patience than Job. I'm thankful for the day he brought his mother home. After losing Amelia, I thought I'd be alone for the rest of my life. She's brought me so much happiness over the past several years. She's a good woman. She deserves better than the likes of my grumpy old ass.

"Grandpa, I'd sure like one of those cookies right about now."

I push my old body off the rock to a standing position. "Come on, I'll take you back to the house."

When I go to put him on the horse, he's soaking wet and shivering. I take off my jacket and put it on him, rolling up the sleeves. "I don't need you catching a cold. Your momma wouldn't' be happy," I tell him.

I get on behind him. As we make our way back, my chest feels heavy again. I halt the horse. "Grandpa needs to check on a few things. You can see the house from here. Do you think you could walk back the rest of the way by yourself like a big boy?"

"I am big, Grandpa," he says, looking up at me.

I climb down, taking him with me. "I'm just gonna sit by this tree and watch you the whole way. Tell Grandma Winnie I love her, and I'll see her soon."

"Okay, Grandpa," he says, running off.

I lean against the tree and clutch my chest as I sit. Patting down my shirt, I realize River has my jacket on that has my nitro in the pocket. *I'll just sit here and rest a bit until the pain passes.*

"Good morning." Keep it, professional man, I tell myself walking into the cafe of the vineyard. She's all I've thought about since the other night. I kept my hands to myself even though all I wanted to do was make love to her. What we did was even more erotic. I've never shared so much with a woman before. We held hands under the stars, and my heart grew for her. I loved talking to her and listening to her stories. She's the perfect woman for me and who I thought I'd never find.

All is good until Rose turns around, flinging her red hair over her shoulder with a pretty smile on her face. The glimmer in her eyes alone had me wanting to have my hands on her, no more talking.

"Good morning, city boy," she says, looking at my

suit. "Awful formal for these parts. You might want to shed the jacket." I know it's her way of teasing me.

Shrugging out of it, I go to place it on the back of a chair, but she stops me.

"There's a coat rack by the door. We won't be meeting in here, and the cafe opens in an hour." She points.

"Do you have an office on the premises?" I ask while hanging up my blazer.

"I do, but I have work to do while I pick your brain."

Glancing down at my clothes, I ask, "Are we going to be out in the vineyard?"

"To start, we're going to the cellar, then the vines need some attention."

"You're right. I'm not dressed for manual labor."

"There is a pair of men's overalls in the storage area out back. Several of the employees leave them here."

"Overalls, huh?" I hold out my arms. "Do I look like an overall type of guy?"

"Suit yourself. But, if you don't change, you can plan on disposing of that crisp white button-down. The stains will never come out." She half grins.

"Fine. I'll change, but don't you make fun of me," I say loudly.

"I promise." I see her cross her fingers and put them behind her back.

"How is your shoulder?" I ask before I walk out the back door.

"It's sore. It feels better out of the sling." She gently rotates her shoulder.

The overalls are right where she said they'd be. After I unbutton my shirt, I'm left with a white t-shirt. Slipping out of my shoes and slacks, I ease myself into the overalls that look as if they've seen their share of blueberry picking. There are several pairs of work boots by the door. I find my size and put them on. When I come out of the storage room, I'm greeted by Rose waiting on me. Her gaze skims my body again, but this time with heat behind it, not the amusement I was expecting.

"Much better," she says, licking her lips.

"You're the only person I know who likes a man in a pair of overalls as opposed to a man in a suit."

"Oh, trust me, there is a time and place for a suit, but in my opinion, these look much better on you." She giggles.

"There is something seriously wrong with you. In my world, I'd be laughed out of the office."

"Perhaps you're hanging out with the wrong

people." She says over her shoulder as she leads me to the wine cellar.

I shove my hands in my pockets to keep from touching her. The last time I was down here with her, it wasn't but minutes before I had her long legs wrapped around my waist. *Focus, Dodge, focus.* I've got to convince her to sell the vineyard; getting in her panties isn't going to work. Besides, I really like her. I don't want to hurt her.

"This batch should be ready any day now. It was from last year's crop." She places her hand on one of the large wooden barrels. "Daddy wants me to infuse the blueberry wine into whiskey and call it Boone's Brand. He thinks it would sell well."

"That would definitely get you into the international market. Whiskey is a big seller. You could promote it more to women with the blueberry infusion."

"With this barrel being ready, it would only take me about ten days to ferment whiskey." She taps a finger to her chin. "I can work on the label and within two weeks have it."

"I have some overseas contacts I can get in touch with. I'm sure they'd place an order right away."

"Maybe I should market it locally first," she says.

"Look, if you want to grow internationally, this is

the way to do it. You can always reserve a few bottles to serve at the winery, but the bulk of 'Boone's Brand' needs to be shipped along with bottles of your finest wine. Your sales will soar."

"I don't know. I should have a test market first."

I place my hands on her waist. "Come on, baby...I mean Rose. Trust me on this."

"We haven't even tasted the product yet."

"If it's anything like the quality of your wine, it's a no-brainer." I want nothing more than to kiss her right now. I lean in, and she pulls away.

"We need to keep this relationship platonic. I can't give into you." She straightens her spine.

I lift my hands in the air. "I'll play this however you want to, but know this, I really do like you."

"We've agreed to be friends, so let's keep it that way." She sticks out her hand.

"I thought maybe after our night under the stars, you'd changed your mind."

"We have business to tend to," she brushes me off.

"As long as you agree not to shower in front of me again." I grin. "You made it very difficult for me to be a gentleman."

"It's a deal."

Surely she's toying with me. I know she felt what

I felt. I reluctantly shake her hand. I'd much rather see her naked than be her friend.

Her phone rings in the bib of her overalls. She pulls it out and frowns. "I need to take this." She excuses herself to the corner of the cellar and whispers.

Does she have a boyfriend I don't know about? Suddenly, I feel jealous and protective at the same time. I have no claims on her, but I'd like to. What's wrong with me? I came here to do a job. I hate the country. It would never work between the two of us. City boy and cowgirls never mesh for very long. I ignore my internal rant, knowing what I feel for her. She's not like any woman I've ever known. The way I feel about her is deep-seated, and it's been there all along.

When she finishes her call, she walks back over to me. Something is wrong. Her entire demeanor has changed. "Everything okay?"

"Mmm-hmm," she says, with a sniff behind it. "I'm going to order what I need to make the whiskey. I'll meet you in the back forty of the vineyards. The keys to the mule are back in the store room." She starts to walk up the stairs, and I grab her elbow.

"Hey, you can talk to me if something is wrong?"

"I'm fine," she insists, leaving my grasp.

I follow her up the stairs. She takes off toward the cafe, and I snag the keys to the mule from the storage room. I take my time driving through the vineyards. This place is beautiful. Something tugs at my heart, telling me this feels like home. I don't understand it, and I can't justify it. It just is. The more I'm around Rose, the more I fall deeper in love with her. She's such a smart, gorgeous woman, yet she makes herself plain in every way. No makeup, no fancy clothes, but damn, does it look good on her. I've been with some gorgeous women, but none of them were natural beauties like her. They were smart, but most of them conniving. There isn't a dishonest bone in Rose's body.

I reach the back forty and can't help myself from picking the blueberries and placing them in a bucket. It isn't long before I see Rose coming over one of the curves of the valley in an ATV. She gets out, tossing me a pair of gloves. "Your hands will stain if you don't use these."

"Thanks," I say, putting them on.

She works beside me without a word, other than wincing in pain every now and then. Her quietness has me worried. "What else do you need me to help you with?"

"I need to research how to price the overseas market and find the best costs for shipping."

"I can do that." I snap my fingers. "There is one company that I bought and sold. They work with glass and create bottles, among other things. I recall seeing this one that would be perfect to house Boone's Brand."

"Did this company you bought from the original owner bring the new owners a lot of profit?"

"Yes. The original owner had a great concept, but he was struggling to get it off the ground. I saw the potential and sold it to one of my investors before I even purchased it."

"How does that work?"

"I knew the owner needed money. All I had to do was dangle the carrot in front of him. I knew I'd win."

"I don't think the original owner would consider you taking advantage of him a win."

"I didn't take advantage of him. He needed my help," I snark.

"I guess it's all about perspective."

She doesn't trust me, perceiving me as the bad guy. I thought I'd won her over.

She stands. "That's what you want to do here."

I join her on my feet. "That was my original

intent. After coming here"—I look around—"seeing this place and how much it means to you, that's not what I want."

"So, why haven't you hightailed it back to the city?"

"One reason is I promised I'd help you. The other, I'd like to be here to see my nephew be born." Why is she making this so difficult?

"I guess those are good reasons." She shrugs her uninjured shoulder.

I close the gap between us, no longer able to keep my lips from hers. Placing my thumb on her chin, I lift her mouth to mine. "I'm going to kiss you, Rose, with no other intention other than I want to." Leaning in slightly, I wait to see if she's going to resist me. Raising up on her tiptoes, she finishes the distance between us, pressing her lips to mine. Blueberries fill my senses along with her sweet taste. Her body gives into mine for a moment, then she tenses and pulls away.

"I'm sorry," she says, brushing my kiss from her lips. "I can't do this. You and I can't be any more than friends." She rushes over to the ATV and takes off.

I dig the keys for the mule out of my pocket and chase after her. As I park, she's running up the stairs to her place. The door slams before I make it to the top of the stairs.

"Rose!" I bang on her door.

"Go away!" she yells.

"I don't understand. What just happened?"

"I said go away, Dodge!"

I turn in a circle twice, unsure of what to do. "I'll make the call about the bottles and to my connections about buying your product. I'll be back tomorrow, and we can talk about it." I press my ear to the door. "Rose, did you hear me?"

"Yes." I hear her crying.

"Look, whatever I did to upset you, I'm sorry."

"Please just go."

I flatten my palm on the door. "Okay, I'll go, but whatever it is that's bothering you, I'm here whenever you need me." I run to my truck and call my boss.

"I'm not doing this. Rose's vineyard is not for sale and never will be."

"What's the matter, Dodge? Have you lost your touch?"

"I just see things from a different perspective now."

"If you don't close this sell, you're fired."

"Then consider me gone." I hang up the phone.

CHAPTER FIFTEEN

ROSE

*L*ooking out my window, I wait to see Dodge's car disappear from the property.

Grabbing my purse, I rush down the stairs. "Can you handle the lunch crowd?" I ask my employee behind the register.

"Yes. Everything alright?" she asks.

I'm sure I look a mess with puffy red eyes and my hair in disarray. "Call me if things get out of hand." I run to my car and drive as fast as I can to my mother's house using one hand.

Daddy is at the horse track when I drive by and wave. I'm glad he's not home. Parking outside of our house, momma is sitting on the front porch watching River play in the dirt with his trucks.

As soon as she sees me, she knows something

ain't right. She stands, and I walk into her hug. "What's wrong? You're scaring me."

"I got a call from Doc," I sob.

"What did he say?"

"When I fell from the horse, he had me do a mammogram because I was so bruised on my breast he wanted to make sure everything was okay. I had never had one before, so he insisted."

"And?" She pulls back to look me in the eyes.

"They found a lump."

She wipes the tears from my cheek. "Oh, sweetie, it could be nothing. You hit the ground pretty hard."

"I know, and that's what he told me…but."

"He wants to do more testing," she finishes my sentence.

I nod frantically.

"That's a good thing," she tries to convince me.

"What if it's not nothing?" I glance down at my chest. "What if it's cancer?"

"Then we'll face it together."

I take a seat in a rocker and wipe my nose with the back of my hand. "I'm too young. I have my whole life ahead of me. I've not even been in love yet. I can't just cut them off!" I say all in one breath.

"You're getting ahead of yourself. I've never known you to panic."

I stand abruptly. "This is my body, Mom. It's not like some business decision I need to make, like which type of blueberries do I want to grow or which label looks the best!"

She hugs me again to calm me down. "I know, sweetie. You have every right to be upset, but let's take it one day at a time."

I pull back from her. "I'm not doing it."

"You're not doing what?" She frowns.

"I'm not lobbing them off." I wave my hands over my breasts.

"But if it's cancer…"

"I don't care! Who would want me…ever…if I don't look like a woman!"

"Your breasts don't make you a woman, Rose."

"No, but men sure like them."

"You can get fake ones, and they can tattoo nipples on to make them look real."

"How can you say any of this to me! You almost died refusing treatment for your leukemia!"

"That was different. River's life was at stake. Mine didn't matter."

"It mattered to me and Daddy! Yet you decided for us. It almost drove Daddy over the edge, and you would have left me without a mother."

"I'm so sorry. I didn't know you were still angry."

"I'm not angry at you, Mom. I'm angry that I'm twenty-five years old facing the fact that I could have breast cancer."

"It still could be nothing."

"What's going on here?" Daddy's voice blares from atop of a horse in the driveway.

"Please don't tell him," I beg her in a whisper. "Nothing," my voice squeaks.

He hops down from the horse. "Looks like something to me. You never cry."

"It's just men issues," Momma says, wrapping her arm around my shoulder.

"If it's Dodge, I can run his ass out of town."

Poor Dodge, he's been nothing but sweet to me. I feel bad for the way I ran out on him this morning. "No, Daddy, I'm fine. Really," I sniff.

"What are you doing home anyway?" Mom tries to distract him.

"I need my shotgun. Bear says there's a coyote up on the ridge." He picks it up from resting on the porch wall.

Mom calls River to come inside. "I'll fix us some lunch."

Daddy kisses momma and then turns to look at me. "I don't like that you're hiding something from me, but you're a grown woman who can take care of herself. But, know this, if that young man hurts my baby girl, I will put some buckshot in his ass."

"Oh, Daddy, you sound just like Grandpa." I hug his neck.

He marches off the porch, and I go inside and sit at the table with my mother. "Why does everyone think Dodge and I are together?"

"Aren't you?" She pours pink lemonade in my glass.

"No," I huff.

"I'm guessing your daddy thinks so because he said you had red marks on your neck one day out at the vineyard, and Dodge had just left."

I nearly spew my lemonade across the room. "Even if Dodge and I had a...fling, doesn't mean we're a couple."

"It does in your daddy's eyes. Besides, I think you really like Dodge. You just don't want to admit it."

"It doesn't really matter if I do or not if I have cancer. I would never burden him with such a thing, and he wouldn't want a damaged woman."

"You think Dodge is that shallow?"

"Yes, I do. He could have any woman he wants. Why would he pick someone with no...with no boobs?" My tears start falling again.

"I think you're wrong about him."

"Don't matter none. I'm not going to let our relationship grow."

"Because you're scared." It's a statement, not a question.

"I've been afraid of Dodge Anderson since the day I met him."

"You aren't afraid of anything. Why Dodge?"

"Because from the first time I saw him, he threw me off guard. I played it off, but there was something about him that took my breath away in that instant. I swore I'd steer clear of him. I had too many things planned in my life to let a man interfere. I did a good job of staying away from him all these years. He pops back into town, and the first thing I do is let him under my skirt and in my heart."

This time momma spits her lemonade. "Rose!"

"What? You can't tell me you were any different with daddy before you were married." I cock a brow at her.

"You got me there. I couldn't keep my hands off of him." She smiles as if she remembers a moment. Then she pushes her glass away from her. "Does Dodge know how you feel about him?"

"No. I've never told him. I came close the other night, but now I'm glad I didn't."

"He must feel it anytime the two of you are together."

"I don't know how he feels about me. Sometimes I think he likes me, then other times I think he's using me."

"Your daddy says he thinks the boy has it bad for you. He said he can't take his eyes off you, and when he's around you, he puffs his chest out like a protective man claiming his woman."

I stand. "It doesn't matter. When he's done helping me, and Missy has her baby, he'll go back to California. He'll be none the wiser of what happens to me."

"I think you should tell him. See what kind of man he is."

"I'm not telling him, and neither are you." I hold out my hand. "Pinky swear to me you won't say a word to anyone."

She reluctantly crosses her finger with mine. "I swear."

"Thank you."

"I want to go with you for the testing."

"Doc said he'd set it up for the end of the week."

"You let me know. I don't want you going through this by yourself."

"Okay, I will as long as you promise not to worry too much."

"I'm your mother. Of course I'm worried."

"I love you, Momma. Thanks for taking me in all those years ago. You've always treated me as if I were your own."

"You are my own. I love you dearly."

"I better get back to the vineyard. Oh, and tell Daddy, I'm using his idea of the Boone Brand. Dodge and I will have it rolled out in two weeks."

"You need to focus on yourself at the moment. You can postpone the rollout if need be."

I walk to the door after giving River a kiss on the head. "Don't forget, your lips are sealed. You can't tell anyone."

Momma makes a zipping motion over her mouth.

When I get in my car, I pull down the mirror and wipe my tears. For the first time in my life, I feel as if my future is uncertain. One minute, my life is all laid out, the next…well, I may not have a future.

My phone rings as I turn off Whiskey Road onto the main road to town. Tucker's name flashes on my dashboard. Surely, Dodge didn't tell him how mean I was to him.

"Hey, Tucker. Did you and Missy get away okay this morning?"

"She's in labor!" he yells.

"What?"

"We were on our way back to Lexington, and she started having contractions."

"Where are you?

"Were pulled over on highway sixty." I hear Missy scream in the background.

"Did you call 911?"

"Yes, but we're halfway between Salt Lick and Lexington in the middle of nowhere, and the baby is coming."

"You can do this, Tucker. How many horses have you helped birth?"

"This is my wife, not a horse!" he hollers.

"Yes, but it's the same concept."

"Fine, fine. You're right. I can do this." Missy screams again.

"I'll stay on the phone with you." I pull over. Uncle Bear happens to ease up behind me. I watch him in the rearview mirror get out of his truck. I roll down my window and wave him to me.

"Are you broke down?" he asks.

"Get in the passenger side," I tell him. He moseys

around and climbs in. "It's Tucker. He and Missy are on the side of the road, and she's in labor."

He snatches the phone from my hand. "How far apart are the contractions?"

"She says the baby is coming. There's no time between contractions anymore. They're one on top of the other. She didn't tell me she'd been having contractions all night long."

"Hand the phone to Missy," he tells him.

"Daddy," she says, panting.

"Do you feel pressure?"

"Yes," she cries.

"Then it's time to push. Put me on speakerphone."

"Okay," she says. "Tucker's right here."

"I know you keep a blanket in the back seat of your truck. Get it out and ready to catch the baby."

"I don't think I can do this." His voice is frantic.

"I'm afraid you don't have a choice, son. Missy, you hold on before you start pushing."

She lets out a hard gasp. "It hurts so bad."

"I know it does, darling."

"I got the blanket," Tucker states.

"It's just like birthing a foal. Have Missy prop up on her elbows, and you get in position."

"Alright. I can already see the top of the baby's head," he hollers.

"I need you to stay calm. Now is the time to push, Missy."

She groans and holds her breath, then screams.

"I know it hurts, darling, but you need to push again with the next contraction."

"She's pushing," Tucker responds. "His head didn't budge!"

"It's alright. It may take a few more times."

"I need to push again!" Missy screams.

"His head came out a little then went back in." Tucker is in full-out panic mode.

"Next time she pushes, see if you can help his head get through. The cord may be wrapped around his neck," Bear tells him.

"I can't do this. We have to wait on the ambulance," Tucker yells.

"Son, listen to me. I've seen you birth cows that have been upside down and wrapped up with their legs tucked under. You can do this." Bear tries to calm him.

"Another one," Missy screams.

We can't hear anything other than the sound of Missy pushing. "Tucker?" Bear asks.

"Give me a second," he says. "I have his head in

my hand, and I've got my fingers between his neck and the cord."

"Have her back off pushing and ease him out, keeping the cord from suffocating him."

"Here he comes!" Tucker yells.

It's quiet for a moment. "I don't hear the baby crying." I've been holding my breath the entire time.

"Sweep the baby's mouth out," Uncle Bear says.

A second later, the sound of a baby crying blares through the phone. "Oh, thank God." I release my held breath.

"Put him on Missy's belly until a paramedic arrives to cut the cord," Uncle Bear instructs them.

"He's beautiful," Missy sobs.

"How can you tell? He's a bloody mess," Tucker says.

"He's got ten fingers and ten toes. He's perfect," Missy says like a proud momma.

"Snap a picture," I say. I can hear the sound of sirens in the background.

A few seconds later, a picture pops up on my phone. I hand it to Uncle Bear to get his first look at his grandson.

"Damn, he is beautiful."

"The ambulance is here. They're going to take Missy and our son to the hospital."

"Give them both a kiss for me, and tell her that her momma and I are on our way."

"I will. See you when you get here." Tucker ends the conversation.

"Congratulations, Grandpa." I hug him.

"That was a little scary."

"Really? You seemed so calm?"

"I had to be to help Tucker, but on the inside, my guts were in a knot."

He gets out of the car. "Give them both my love and tell them to send lots of pictures."

"Will do."

ROSE

"Iknow I need to have the tests done, Momma, but I've been so busy this week I haven't even given it a second thought. Dodge went to Tucker's, and I've been concentrating on Boone's brand."

"It's been two weeks since Doc called you." She firmly plants her hands on her hips.

"Look at this place. It's busy with people. I can't just take off a disappear for a day." She follows closely behind me out the back door to the cellar.

"I'll cover for you. Just tell me what you need done." She's on my heels down the stairs. "Your dad knows this place almost as well as you do. He could work it for you."

I whirl in her direction. "You didn't tell him, did you?"

"No. I promised I wouldn't, but he knows something's up with you."

I take a small cup off one of the open shelves and fill it halfway full of the whiskey. "Try this." I hand it to her.

"Is this Boone's Brand." She holds it under her nose, smelling it.

"Yes. It turned out better than I could've even imagined."

She takes a sip. "Wow, this is fantastic."

"I know, right."

"Has your grandpa tried this? He's the whiskey connoisseur."

"He hasn't yet, but when I told him about it, he said he'd come out here today on his way back from seeing his great-grandson. He'll drop Winnie off at the ranch before he heads over."

"I'm honestly surprised you didn't drive to Lexington to see your new nephew."

"Missy and I have been FaceTiming a lot. Morgan is the cutest little thing."

"Are you avoiding spending time with Dodge?"

"We've been on the phone several times strategizing the marketing of the whiskey." I don't want to tell her that I've been short and to the point because I am avoiding any in-depth conversation with him, even though he asks me every time what's wrong.

"When's he coming back to the vineyard?"

"I'm sure this week. The bottles and labels we ordered are due in today. He'll want to see them, then I'm guessing he'll head back to California."

"Is that what you want?"

"Yes. I've got enough to deal with." I head up the stairs.

"I really wish you'd go see Doc." Her feet stomp like an angry woodpecker on the wooden steps.

"I will when I have time." I shut and lock the cellar door.

"I know you're busy, but please, do it for me...for your father. I'm worried about you."

"Well, you need to stop. I feel perfectly fine. Like you said, it was from the fall. My shoulders almost a hundred percent." I move my arm up and down to show her.

She takes her hands, placing them on either side of my face. "I love you, but I need to know that you're okay."

"I'll follow up with him. Just give me a few more weeks to get Boone's Brand going."

"Fine. I don't like you waiting, but I can't force

183

you to move any quicker. But, don't think I won't remind you." She shakes a finger at me.

"I have no doubt you'll put it in your calendar, and I get a call."

She pulls out her cellphone doing just that. "Thanks for the idea."

"There's two of my favorite girls," Grandpa says, walking toward us.

"You're back early," I say, glancing at my watch.

"We left around six this morning. Winnie wanted to get back and open up the shop."

"How is Morgan?" Momma asks him.

"He's the cutest thing I've seen in a long time." He hugs me. "You're next on the list for a baby," he says.

"Shoot me now. No babies for me," I snort, "unless it's my wine babies."

"Speaking of which, where is that whiskey? Winnie had a tight rein on me at the Anderson Ranch." He loops his fingers through his belt loops on his jeans.

I take out the key, unlocking the cellar. "Momma just took a sip and loved it."

"It is really good. I've got to go pick up River and take him for his follow-up appointment. I'll catch up with you later," she tells Grandpa.

"Follow me," I say, opening the door.

"I've been meaning to tell you how proud I am of you. This place is awesome and a gold mine, I'm sure."

"I don't know about the gold mine, but I do believe this whiskey will be a hit." I take down another cup and start to pour it. I stop when it's halfway full, and Grandpa reaches over and tips the bottle, filling it the rest of the way.

"Good thing Grandma Winnie isn't here." I giggle.

"What she don't know won't hurt her." He presses the cup to his lips for a sip, then tilts his head back, gulping it down. "Damn, that's good." He holds out the cup for another refill.

"You aren't just saying that because I'm your granddaughter, are you?"

"Sweetheart, I'd tell you if it tasted like shit. If nothing else, I'm an honest man."

"That you are." I fill his cup again.

"Dodge told me he's been working on a marketing plan for you. Sounds like, with his help, you'll have backorders in no time. I'm thinking he's got it bad for you."

"Don't be silly. We're doing business together. That reminds me, I need to pay him for his time."

"Oh, that should go over well." He chuckles.

"Why do you say that? He came here on business."

"I think his purpose on being here changed when he saw you."

"Don't be ridiculous. It's business, nothing more."

"Suit yourself. How about more of that whiskey?" He holds out his cup.

"One last bit. I don't want Grandma Winnie shutting me down before I even have it bottled," I snicker.

"I'll be expecting a bottle of my own," he winks at me.

"How are you feeling, Grandpa? I think your color is a little off." I tilt my head to get a good look at him.

"Nothing major. A few twinges of old age creaking in my bones, that's all. I'm too ornery for anything else. Oh, before I forget to warn you, Dodge left the same time we did this morning. My gut tells me he'll be headed here to see you."

"I didn't think he'd be back for another week?" I instinctively run my hands through my long hair, trying to spruce it up.

He gut-laughs. "I ain't ever seen a woman fixing her hair unless there is a man involved."

"I need to get back to my office and run some

numbers before he shows up." I playfully nudge him up the stairs. As my feet hit the top, I see Dodge's car. He's pulling around to the back. He jumps out and runs up the stairs to my space.

"I'd say that boy is looking for you" Grandpa points out. "If you want me to run him off, I will, but he's kinda grown on me the last couple of weeks. You should've seen him with Morgan. He was a big help on the ranch, so Tucker had extra time with Missy and his son. For a man to be a city boy, he's damn good with the horses and the cattle."

"Sounds like you have a bromance with him." I poke him with my elbow.

"I don't know what the hell that means, but you should give him a chance."

I roll my eyes. "I don't need a man, Grandpa. I'm doing just fine on my own."

"If you say so, kiddo." He wraps his arm around my shoulder and kisses my temple.

Dodge comes running back down the stairs and shades his hands over his brow, and glances around the property. As soon as he sees me, he takes off in a jog, headed in my direction.

"Come by the house for a visit," Grandpa says, walking away.

"There you are," Dodge huffs, a little winded.

"I'm glad you're here. Walk with me to my office," I say casually, leading the way.

"The shipment of bottles will be here before the end of the day. I received a copy of the label, and it looks great." He takes out his phone to show me a picture.

"Yeah, the designer emailed me a copy yesterday. I approved it already." We walk to a shed, and I open the door.

"This is your office? I thought this was for storage." He walks in behind me, looking around. "From the outside, this ain't much, but it looks nice. You kept the same theme as your place, but I'm sure there were other spaces for an office."

"I like it out here. No one bothers me." I sit behind the wooden desk that my dad made for me out of a falling tree. I love the rugged look of wood. I pull out my checkbook from a drawer and start writing. "I know we didn't have an agreed-upon amount, but this should cover your time." I rip it out, handing it to him.

He looks at it, then at me. "I don't want your money." His forehead creases as he tosses it back on my desk.

"I didn't expect you to work for free."

"I have a job," he snarls, making his way to my

side of the desk. "What happened that day in the cellar? After you took that phone call, your attitude towards me changed." He leans on the edge of my desk.

I bite my bottom lip, contemplating what to tell him. "Nothing that would ever concern you."

He squats, taking my hands in his. "I care about you, Rose, more than I care to admit. I know we agreed to be friends, but every time I think about you, my heart does this little flip-flop thing. I didn't understand at first. I thought back to when we met all those years ago, and it did the same thing then. I want to explore what's between us, but you fight me every step of the way."

"We live in two different worlds. It would never work."

"But, what if I wanted to try and make it work?" His gaze bounces back and forth with mine.

"My life is here. I'm never moving to California, and long-distance relationships don't work."

"What if I move here?"

"To Salt Lick?" My voice rises a few octaves. "What about your job?"

"I can work anywhere."

I free my hands of his and tap my nails on my desk. "So you're still working your original motive.

You want me to fall head over heels in love with you so you can sell my company."

He stands abruptly. "One thing you need to understand, I never had any plans on falling in love with you. That part just happened. Secondly, I told my boss I wouldn't be working the deal, and the vineyard wasn't and never would be for sale."

My mind reels with what he said. He loves me? I choose to play it off and only focus on the last part. "You really told them it wasn't for sale?"

He lifts an eyebrow. "Did you hear the first part? I'm in love with you, Rose."

"I heard you, but I'm not looking for a relationship." I can't burden him with my issues. Besides, once he found out, he'd turn and run.

"I wasn't either, but it doesn't change how I feel about you." He snakes his hands around my waist, lifting me to my feet. "You can deny it all you want, but I know you have feelings for me too."

"How do you know that?" I keep my gaze glued to his.

"Because when I do this, I feel your body melting into mine."

He kisses me hard, and he's right; I melt. His hand at the back of my neck draws me closer. Our tongues dance a beautiful dance together.

He lifts me, setting me on the desk. He draws back, pressing his forehead to mine. "Tell me you want this as badly as I do." His voice is raspy and low.

Taking his hand, I place it on my breast, and for a split second, I want to jump out of my own skin, by I reign it in, wanting to feel his hands on me. He squeezes, and I moan as my fingers undo his belt. With my other hand, I cup him. "You're hard," I groan.

"And, I'm betting anything you're wet." His teeth nip at the tender skin of my neck.

A knock at the door has us both panting. "Ignore it," he grates.

"I can't. The vineyard is open for business." I hop off the desk and fix my top. I hear his belt fastening as I open the door.

"Sorry to bother you, but there's a shipment here. The driver says it needs to be unloaded." It's one of the workers who helps with berry picking.

"Thank you," I say. "Tell him I'll be right there."

Dodge walks up behind me. "I'll unload it for you, and then I'll come back to finish what we started."

As much as I want to scream yes, I don't. "I let things get out of hand. As soon as our business is done, so are we." I know it's harsh, but I'm doing it to protect him.

"Evidently, you don't know me very well. I don't give up easily," he says as he walks by me to go unload the truck.

"*B*rian Long claims his car was stolen over a month ago," Mike sighs into the phone.

"Did he file a police report on it when it happened?" I ask.

"Yes, he did."

"Did you inquire as to whether he has any affiliation with Rossi?"

"There is no link between the two men. You're grasping at straws, Ethan. There is no sign of him."

"Alright, I'll back down as long as you're sure."

"Look, I'd like to find Rossi for you to put your mind at peace, but the simple truth is, he's fallen off the face of the earth. If he doesn't want to be found, he surely wouldn't show his face here."

"He would if he thought I'd let my guard down."

"You haven't. Stay alert, but you have to find a way to not let this consume you."

"I only want to protect my family."

"From the sight of Jane at the shooting range, I'd say she's more than capable of taking care of herself." He chuckles. "She's a better shot than a few of my men. I should ask her to join the police force."

"Stay away from my wife." I laugh. "Thanks for getting back to me. Let me know if anything changes."

"You know I will, man."

I leave the police station and head back to my office. Tally is coming out of my office when the elevator doors open. "There you are," she says, waving a file. "I thought you were still barricaded in your office."

"I had a personal errand to run." I take the file from her. "What's this?"

"It's the city budget along with notes from the board."

"You know I don't get involved with numbers." I move past her.

"Well, you need to take a look. It appears someone is trying to push you out of this position to hire someone for less pay."

I hang my hat on the hook and plop down in my office chair, opening the file. "If they can find someone to do this job for less money, then I say go right ahead." I skim the numbers. "Whose suggestion was this based on?"

"He's the new guy out of Utah. He's an investor for cattle purchases for larger ranches."

I close the file. "Hopefully, you squashed it."

"Of course I did. I told them you were the best livestock agent in the entire southeast." She sits, crossing one leg over the other.

"Then why did you bother showing me this?"

"I thought you needed to know, that's all." The corner of her mouth angles downward as she shrugs. "I know you've been looking over your shoulder lately for Rossi. Perhaps he has something to do with it."

"Did you find a connection between the two of them?" I lean forward in my seat.

"Other than the fact that he's from Rossi's home-town, no. It could be a coincidence."

"I'll have Mike run a background check on him."

She stands. "Don't worry, I won't let them give your job to anyone else. You're far too valuable."

My hair stands on end, watching her leave my office. She's up to something, but why would she help me if she was? Is she trying to throw me off her scent? I scan the document from the file, listing the guy's name, address, and phone number, then email to Mike, asking him to do a detailed search on him. Finishing up my day, I head to the ranch. I promised my mother I'd come by and see her when she called to let me know they were back from Tucker and Missy's place.

I'm greeted in the doorway with a hug like she hadn't seen me in forever. "I missed you."

"Missed you, too, Mom."

"I have tons of pictures to show you. Morgan is the sweetest little baby," she says, taking my hand and leading me to the dining room.

I sit, and she pours two glasses of iced tea. "Where's Chet?"

"He said there was a fence that needed mending."

"Whatever you're cooking smells heavenly. That's odd about Chet. He has men to repair fences."

"It's a roast. You're welcome to stay for dinner. It seemed odd to me too. He was acting kinda weird for him. He kissed my cheek and told me how much he loves me and said he'd see me soon."

"Jane said she's cooking tonight."

"Call her and tell her to wrap it up for tomorrow night. I'd love to see her and Mercy."

"It's been a long day, Mom. I want to go home, kick my feet up, have a cold beer, and enjoy my wife and daughter."

She scoots her chair next to mine and clicks through the pictures on her phone. "Missy is happier than I've ever seen her. And that Tucker, he's going to be such a good daddy. He didn't want to ever give him up for someone else to hold."

Boone comes walking in the back door. "Hey, Ethan. Winnie." He opens the fridge and pops open a beer.

"I was just showing Ethan all the pictures of the baby." She holds up her phone, and Boone scrolls through them. "Good-looking, kid. Takes after the Calhouns." He hands it back to her. "Where's the old man? He called me earlier and said he wanted to take a look at the new cattle."

"He's still not back." She glances at her watch. "He's been gone for a while."

"Mom said he went out to mend a fence." A worry seats itself in my chest. "How long has it been?" I ask her.

"A couple hours now."

"I'll go check on him. Did he happen to say where the fence was down?" Boone sets his beer on the table and ambles toward the back door.

"He said it was just past the barn, near the big oak tree."

"I'm glad you enjoyed your visit, Mom." I want to distract her until Boone comes back.

"I did. It was good for Chet too. He loves the babies."

"He spoils Mercy rotten." I chuckle. "He was reading to her, and there was a lamb in the book, and Mercy was fixated on it. He told her when she turned three, he'd buy her one."

"I'm sure he will too." She laughs, then a worry line mares her brow. "Maybe I should go help Boone find Chet." She starts to stand, but I stop her.

"I'll go. You stay here and keep an eye on your roast." I get up and head out the screen door. Checking the barn first, there is no sign of him. His horse is still in the stall. I walk through the back of the barn and glance up the hill at the old oak tree. Boone is sitting on the ground next to Chet, who's slumped over to one side. Slowly, I move toward them. Boone's head falls against the tree, and I see his chest heaving. I know the instant I look at Chet, he's gone. I go to my knees with heartache.

"He's not been gone long," Boone sniffs.

"Why the hell did he come out here?" Tears fill my vision.

"I think he knew, and he didn't want to die in front of your mother. He wanted us to find him."

"How is this family supposed to manage without you?" I touch the toe of his boot. "You're the glue for all of us."

"He taught all of us how to run this place and protect our family." Boone wipes his face with his hand.

"The first time I met the old man, I was terrified of him. Once he warmed up to me, he treated me like a son."

"He took my sorry ass in and did the same for me. I could never repay him for the love he showed me."

I get off the ground and hold out my hand to Boone, helping him up. "He always told me and my mother how much you meant to him."

Boone squats and puts one arm around Chet's neck and the other under his knees, lifting him. "I'm going to take him to the barn while you tell your mother."

I follow him, watching Boone place Chet in the stall with his favorite horse. Taking a deep breath in and clearing the sob filling my chest, I head to the main house, knowing damn good and well this is going to devastate my mother.

"Did you find him?" my mother asks when my boots hit the hardwood floor in the kitchen.

"We did," I say softly, stepping toward her.

"Tell him he needs to get washed up. Dinner will be ready soon." She places an oven mitt on her hand.

I close the distance between us and take the mitt off, placing my hands on her shoulders. "Mom, come sit." I pull out a chair at the table.

Her eyes finally meet mine, and she swallows hard. "There's something wrong, isn't there?" She sits.

I take the seat next to her, scooting it so I can face her. "Boone found Chet resting against the big oak tree."

"Resting...as in napping?" Tears glisten in the corners of her eyes.

"He's gone, Momma."

"It's not true." Her hand covers her mouth.

"I'm so sorry."

She sobs in my arms. "Why didn't he stay here with me. Maybe I could have done something to save him." Her head bobs on my chest.

"I think he knew it was his time, Momma. He didn't want to burden you. He knew you'd try to save him."

She stands abruptly. "I want to see for myself."

"Boone moved him to the barn."

She swings open the door, and I stay close beside her. She hesitates outside the barn door as I hold it open for her. Her hands are wringing together in front of her. "You don't have to do this right this minute," I say.

She sucks up her tears and lifts her chin. "I do." She walks over to the stall, where she sees Boone. He yanks the hat off his head and holds the door open for her. His eyes are bloodshot, and his face is filled with grief.

Momma walks in and sits in the hay next to Chet. She takes his hand and places it in her lap. "What have you gone and done?" she weeps. "You should've told me you weren't feeling well, you old coot!" I can barely watch as tears roll down her cheeks onto her dress. "What am I going to do without you? We haven't had enough time together." She kisses his forehead. "I love you so much."

I gingerly sit beside her. "He knew how much we all loved him."

"Are you sure? 'Cause there were days he made me so angry," she cries.

I wrap my arm around her shoulder, holding her close. "He made all of us angry a time or two, but he knew."

"What am I going to do without him?" she sobs.

"I'm going to take care of you. You won't be alone."

Boone steps inside the stall. "Do you want me to tell the rest of the family, or do you want to do it?" he asks my mom.

"I don't think I can say the words," she cries harder.

"I'll take care of it." Boone wipes his nose on his sleeve. "I'll call a family meeting. This isn't something I want to tell them over the phone." He walks out of the barn.

I sit with my mother as she cries, talking to Chet. A few minutes later, Boone pops his head in the stall. "They're all on their way. I told them we had an emergency on the ranch, and we needed all hands on deck. I told them to meet me in the house."

"Do you want to stay here?" I ask my mother.

She nods.

"I'll stay with you then," I say.

"No. I'd like some time alone with him before everyone shows up. You go, I'll be okay."

I stand and walk out with Boone to the house.

I hear Bear pull up on the ATV, and he bursts through the door. "What's going on? I didn't hear of anything happening on the ranch."

"I'll explain when everyone else arrives," Boone tells him.

Twenty minutes later, Wyatt is the last to arrive. Jane has been nagging me to tell her. "Wait, where's Daddy? He's always in charge of these meetings."

"That's why we're here. Chet copped a squat by the old oak tree on the hill and never woke up," Boone chokes out.

Ellie stands and immediately stomps toward the back door, followed by Clem and Rose. Jane is on their heels with Nita and Molly.

"I moved him into the barn," Boone hollers after them.

Noah's eyes flood with tears. "I was on the phone with him earlier today."

Bear looks as if he's in shock, and Wyatt is stoic.

"I need to call Margret," he says, stepping out onto the porch.

"Missy needs to know." Bear takes out his phone and heads to Chet's office.

"I can't believe he's gone," Ian sniffs.

One by one, except for Wyatt, we make our way to the barn. The women are all gathered around my mother, telling stories. They're laughing through their tears.

"I've always been told the last thing to go is hearing. I wanted Chet to hear how much he was loved," my mother says, trying to smile.

"He was very loved." Clem touches my mother's arm.

"I'm so grateful for the time we had together," Mom whimpers.

"After Momma died, I didn't think the cranky cowboy would find anyone to love him like Momma did. I was wrong. You made him happy, and he loved you very much," Clem assures her.

Jane chimes in. "I only knew Amelia by the stories that were told and through the love in her children's eyes. The one thing I know is that I saw that same love for you flowing through each and every one of us."

Mom blows her nose in a tissue Nita hands her. "I have no doubt how much he loved me and each and every one of you. He told me as much every day."

I glance around, and Wyatt is still not here. "I'm going to go check on Wyatt," I say before walking back to the house. I find him on the porch swing where the old man would enjoy his evenings. He's staring out at the land. Taking a seat in the rocker, I sit quietly for a moment.

"You alright?"

When he speaks, it's then I realize he's crying. "We need to decide where his body will rest."

"He told my mother he wanted to be buried next to Amelia."

"She's okay with that?" he chokes.

"Yes. She'll honor his wishes."

"There were days I wanted to strangle him…" his words drop off for a second. I wait for him to regain his composure. "But, I'd have given my life for the man. He wasn't always the best father, yet he was an honorable man to his family. He was hard on us growing up because he wanted each of us to be strong when we grew up and had our own families. He saved my sorry ass more than once."

"You did the same for him. He told my mother how proud he was of you. You conquered your addiction, and it changed your life for the better."

He stands. "I will miss him until the day I die." I've never seen Wyatt come undone. His hand shakes as he reaches for the screen door. "It's my job now to take care of things."

CHAPTER EIGHTEEN

WYATT

y father's death has rocked me to the core. I've always considered myself a strong man when it comes to emotions, but I can't seem to stop the tears once they start. I have to gain control today if I'm going to get through his eulogy. My dad, even in his death, is a little bossy. He wanted only family and the gathering to be on the hill where our mother is buried, where he will be laid to rest.

I watch and listen as the family arrives. Rose is sobbing, saying she can't believe he's gone. Only a few hours earlier that day was she talking to him. I think every one of us is in disbelief, especially Winnie. Ethan says he thinks she's in shock. We've all made sure to tell her it doesn't change our relationship with her. As far as we're concerned, she's a Calhoun.

Margret squeezes my hand. "It's time, sweetie."

I blink back the tears, clear my throat and stand in front of everyone. "The loss of our father is one of the most difficult things each of us has had to endure since our mother died. We were lucky to have him as an example. Mind you, I didn't always feel this way, but good or bad, he was a major influence in my life and each of his children's lives. He wasn't a saint by any stretch of the imagination.

"Daddy truly believed if you worked hard, took care of your family, and with a little luck from God, you'd have a good life. He proved this with his family and the land. He may not have said it enough in his younger years, but he was proud of each of us. He adored all of his grandchildren, and thankfully, he got to meet the newest member of our family." I glance over at Missy, who is hugging her baby with tears streaming down her cheeks.

"He showed strength, an orneriness right up until the end." They laugh through their heartache. "The other thing he gave us was hope. No matter what our situation was, Daddy always came through with a piece of advice that offered something better. I love him for that." I look down at Margret. "I can only pray that when I die, my wife and children can share funny stories about me and talk about how much I was loved and respected. If that's the case, then like my father, I will have led a complete life.

"There are pieces of our father he left behind for all of us. I will never be able to look at this land without knowing the sacrifices he made so many times to fight for this land. He did this for his legacy to leave us and his love of the ranch. We all have sweat equity in it. From the time we could walk, he taught us how to work the land, sharing his knowledge his father passed down to him. Every single one of us has ownership in this place, including Morgan. It's what our father wanted, and it will be handed down for many generations. I will see to it."

I turn to face Winnie. "You gave our father unconditional love after our mother died. As far as I'm concerned, you're the saint. As much as we all loved him, he was a pain in the ass most of the time. But you made him happy, and he changed some of his ways. He told us he loved us and made sure we knew it, and for that, I'm grateful."

"We all are," Ellie says.

"Yes, I agree," Clem supports her.

"So on this day, clear blue sky, with the wind blowing at our backs, we honor him and say good-bye. We love you, Daddy."

One by one, we each say our goodbyes as his casket is lowered to the ground next to our mother.

CHAPTER NINETEEN

ROSE

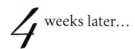 weeks later…

"Damn it, Rose!" Daddy's voice booms in my office, echoing off the steel walls.

"Well, good morning to you too, Daddy." I'm not sure what has his feathers ruffled like one of the angry roosters.

"Why haven't you had your testing done?"

My eyes squint. "Momma told you?"

"Yes. She should've told me weeks ago. I take that back. You should've told me." He's leaning over my desk, pointing his calloused finger at me.

"I have a right to privacy, and Momma and I are

going to have words. She promised not to say anything to you."

"She held that promise as long as she could. Your mother has begged you to go get your tests done."

"More like nagged!"

He stands tall, throwing back his shoulders. "She loves you and wants you to take care of yourself."

I've never gone toe to toe with my daddy, and I ain't starting now. "I've been busy, that's all. The sales of Boone's Brand have been more than I could have anticipated, and with Grandpa dying, well, I just ain't had time to think about myself."

"That stops now. I will deal with the sales. You pick up the phone and make the appointment." He's pointing and yelling again.

"Fine. I will."

He crosses his arms over his chest. "I'll wait."

"Oh, you mean right this minute? I've got to finish what I'm doing. I'll make a mental note to call later."

"Rose." His voice is deep and menacing. Disapproval gleams in the wrinkles at the corner of his eyes.

His gaze is so penetrating I force myself to pick up the phone. I clutch it in my hand, staring at it.

"Do you need me to give you the phone number?"

A twinge of frustration is laced in his voice. And, an infinitesimal twitch in his cheek tells me he has hit his limit of patience with me.

A groan accompanies my eye roll as I dial the number to Doc's office. I make the appointment with the receptionist. "There, you happy now?"

"Yes. Thank you." A hushed tone wedges itself between his words.

"You tell Momma, I ain't too pleased with her."

"I'll do no such thing. She's only doing her job. She's been worried about you."

I blow out a long, frustrated breath. "I know."

"Write down the appointment time and date." He tosses me a pen from my desk.

"Why, so you can check up on me?"

"I'm going with you."

"No, you are not!" I drum my fingernails on my desk.

"Either I'm going or your mother. Take your pick." He sloughs off a lame shrug.

"Being that I'm not speaking to my mother at this moment, I guess I'm stuck with you." I scribble the date and time on a piece of paper.

Handing it to him, he glances at it then shoves it in his pocket. "I'll be picking you up to take you."

"You don't trust me to go?" I blink owlishly.

"Nope."

"How did I go from an independent grown woman to feeling like I'm three years old within a matter of minutes?"

He rolls his shoulders to obviously relieve his tension. "You are one of the most responsible people I know with everyone but yourself. You work from sun up to sundown, some days not even eating."

"I eat." He cocks a brow. "Okay, maybe I get distracted and skip and meal or two," I relent.

"I know you're scared." He walks over to my side of the desk. "But, you can't ignore it."

"That's what Grandpa did. He took his nitro and pretended nothing was wrong." I get choked up on the thought.

Daddy leans down and lifts me up by the shoulders. "I don't want that to happen to you." He draws me in for a tight much-needed hug. "I miss him too."

"I'm sorry, Daddy. I don't want you and Momma to worry about me."

"Thank you for the apology. I think you owe someone else those words."

I pull back from him. "Who?"

"Dodge."

"Dodge?" I wrinkle my nose.

"I've watched the two of you working together

these past several weeks. You've been cold and distant to him."

"Oh, so now you want me to like him?"

"What I want is for you to follow your heart. For whatever reason, you've been keeping him at arm's length, and he's walking around like a little lost puppy dog."

I jerk free of his grasp. "So, it doesn't matter to you that he's using me?"

"How is he using you, darling?"

"He only wants to grow my company so he can convince me to sell it so he can make a fortune selling it to one of his investors."

"He told me about that. It was true in the beginning. After he spent time with you, he told his boss to take a hike."

"He quit his job? Why didn't he tell me?"

"Dodge wanted you to trust him to do the right thing."

I grab the armrests of my chair and sit. "I was the one using him in the end. I wanted his help, thinking he'd still try to talk me into selling."

He squats in front of me. "Do you love him?"

"I don't think I've let myself go there."

"Don't close your heart off to something that

could bring you happiness. I know you love this place, but it won't keep you warm at night."

Placing my hand on his cheek, I smile sweetly and say, "You've always been a hopeless romantic."

He chuckles. "Don't tell anyone. It will tarnish my badass reputation with my men."

"Your secret is safe with me." I make a cross-motion over my heart.

He stands. "I don't think I'm going to forget this appointment." He holds the paper in the air then stuffs it in his denim jacket pocket, heading out the door.

I finish the email I was working on before daddy found me, shut my computer down then head to the cafe to check on things. As usual, there's a line out the door. I know most everyone that comes here from town unless Jane has sent them over from the Magnolia. There is a man in line with a dark suit, shades, and slick-looking shoes. His hair matches the color of his attire, and his shoulder is lifted, holding on to his cell phone as he flips through a notebook he's holding. He looks like a fish out of water, even different from the visitors who come from the Magnolia.

Putting on an apron, I step up to help at the counter, taking orders. The guy nudges his dark glasses down his nose and stares at me. He tells whomever he's speaking to he has to go.

"May I help you?" I ask him when he's next in line.

"Are you Rose Methany?"

"Who might be asking?"

"I'm a...friend of Dodge Anderson."

My instincts tell me not to trust this man.

"Nice to meet you...friend of Dodge's. What can I get for you?"

"I'd like to have a moment of your time if that's possible."

"As you can see, I motion with my head, "we're a little busy at the moment. You can make schedule a time to see me." I motion for the next person in line.

"Wait," the man says. "I'll have a bottle of Boone's Brand and a turkey sandwich."

Now I know something is up. I haven't advertised the whiskey locally, only through internet sales overseas. "I'm sorry, Boone's Brand isn't available, but I can sure fix you that turkey sandwich." His smirk makes me feel like a hornet stung me on the backside. "Anything else?"

"I think I'll hang around and see if the crowd lets up to meet with you."

"Suit yourself." I have no plans on discussing anything with him.

He mutters something to himself, then shuffles his feet like a petulant child, knowing I have no intention of giving him what he wants.

When the midmorning rush is under control, I slip out the back while mister hoity-toity sips his coffee. I run upstairs, change into my work clothes, and hop on one of the ATVs.

"Ms. Methany!" I hear coming from behind me.

It's him. Dang it. "I'm still busy," I say, trying to brush him off.

"I have an offer for you that I don't think you're going to want to miss out on." He's sucking in air from running.

"How do you know about Boone's Brand, and what did you say your name was?"

"My name is Bellamy. I'm Dodge's boss."

My laugh comes out haughty. "Don't you mean his ex-boss? I heard he quit."

"I don't know where you gathered your information from. How did you think I'd know about Boone's Brand if he wasn't still working for me?" A smug grin is perched on his lips, making him look like a vulture.

I un-straddle the ATV, spin around to face him,

and draw up my fists like angry stones. "You need to get the hell off my property."

"Damn, no wonder Dodge likes you so much. You're a challenge for him. Usually, the pretty ladies fall at his feet with a simple smile from him."

"All you're gonna get is a bloody nose if you don't get out of here." He tries to hand me the file he's been gripping, and I knock it out of his hand.

He squats, picking up the papers that flew out. "I'm offering you ten times what this place is worth."

"You wouldn't be offering if you didn't think it was worth more. Now, use the ears the good Lord gave you and hear me when I tell you to get off my land and never come back."

He steps toward me, and I take a swing at him only to find my feet being lifted off the ground and someone holding me by the waist.

"What the hell, Rose?" Dodge says.

"Put me down!" I holler, scratching at his arms.

"He'll charge you with assault." He holds me tighter.

"I don't give a donkey's butt! I want him off my property!"

"Bellamy, you should go unless you want me to release her on you. I'm sure somewhere around here she has a shotgun stashed."

"Fine. I'll leave, but she needs to see this offer when she calms down," he says.

"Calm down! I'll show you calmed down!" I try to free myself from Dodge's hold, but it's no use.

"Get out of here," Dodge roars.

He doesn't let me go until the man is out of sight. "Let me loose!" I kick at his shins. Dodge sets me on my feet, and I nearly topple over trying to face him. "You need to go back where you came from!"

He lifts his hands in the air as if he's surrendering. "Why are you so angry at me?"

"Number one, you didn't let me kill him! Two, you're in cahoots with him."

"I'm not, Rose. I swear. I quit working for him shortly after I got here."

I plant my feet in front of him and almost bump my nose with his. "Then how did he know about Boone's Brand?"

"He probably read about it on the international market. Your name and the winery are all over the place. It's his job to know what's out there."

I stomp off back toward my place. "I don't believe you!" When my foot hits the first landing, I glance over my shoulder. Dodge has both hands in his hair tugging at it. He must've taken off in a run after me because, by the time I get my door open, he's shoving me inside, slamming the door behind him.

"I am not working for Bellamy. Every hour of every day I've put in this place is because...well, damn it, Rose...is because I'm in love with you. Sometimes I think I'm insane. You're hard-headed, stubborn..."

"I think those two things mean the same thing," I interrupt him.

"Can be downright mean at times, and you've been cold as ice."

"Then you're right. You're insane."

He snags my hand, pulling me toward him. "Then call me crazy, but I've fallen for everything about you." His lips crash hard on mine.

I can't breathe from letting him explore my mouth. It's sweet and bitter at the same time. He draws back, resting his forehead against mine. "You are one maddening woman."

I twine my fingers at the nape of his neck. "We can't do this, Dodge. We're too different, and we live worlds apart."

"That's just it. We aren't. I thought I loved the city life, but I was only running from my past. I didn't want to end up like my father." He breaks our connection and leads me to the couch. "Thing is, I'm more like him than I ever wanted to admit. When I go back to the family ranch, I feel alive. The horses feel like home. You made me see what I was missing. I'm ashamed of some of the things I've done, and I don't want to be that man anymore. I want to be the type of man you can fall in love with. Is that possible, Rose?"

I pace in front of him. "I don't know how I feel. I haven't let myself feel anything for anyone ever other than my family."

"Admit it, you and I have had a connection since the day we met."

"I ain't saying we didn't. There were so many other things I wanted."

He stands in front of me, stopping my movement. "You can have both now. It's up to you. I ain't going anywhere."

My head is spinning. Momma said he wasn't shallow, now's the time to test him. "You say you love me, right?"

"Yes." His answer is firm and unwavering.

"Would you still love me if I had no boobs?"

"What? His brow furrows.

"I have a lump in my breast, and I need a test done. If I have cancer, chances are they might remove my breasts." A large lump builds in my throat from saying the words out loud.

"Oh, Rose, I'm so sorry." He hugs me. "You must be terrified."

"You didn't answer my question," I move out of his arms.

"I'd love you if you were blind, one-legged, bald, and had no teeth. Well, maybe not the no teeth part," he teases.

I'm truly stunned by his answer. "Really?"

He places his hand over my heart. "I love the person on the inside, Rose. If you'll let me, you and I can face this together."

I press my fingertips on my temples to stop the ache. "I want to believe what you're telling me, but you yourself said you didn't want to settle down and have a family. Now all of a sudden you've changed your mind?"

"I didn't propose, Rose." He chuckles. "You need time to fall in love with me, and when you do, yes, I want it to be just you and I."

"No kids?"

"No kids. Just you and me."

"Can I have a hot minute to think about it?"

Sadness fills his eyes. "You need time to decide how you feel about me."

I place my hand on his cheek. "I do know we've

had a connection from the beginning. I've fought it, just like you did. I do love you, Dodge." I kiss him this time, but I don't let it take over. "I don't want to burden you with my troubles. Please give me time to work through it."

"You'd never be a burden to me, Rose, but I'll do as you ask."

CHAPTER TWENTY

JANE

"I'm so glad Nita and Molly agreed to cover the bed-and-breakfast for the day. It's been so busy. The break is nice." I push Mercy in a stroller as we make our way to the market in Farmers, Kentucky. We come here to stock up on fruits and vegetables for the Magnolia. Plus, we love to check out all the new jellies and jams, along with other trinkets.

"I love getting to spend time outside of work with you and this little one." Margret wheels along next to us.

"When we get inside the barn, I'll take out your walker so you can stretch your legs. I tucked it into the bottom of the stroller."

"I'd like that. The physical therapist said I need to start using it more and more each day."

When we reach the barn, I pull it out, trying not to wake up Mercy from her nap. She's a bear if she doesn't get her sleep in.

Margret unlatches the sides of the folded walker and pulls herself up. Her braces on her legs clink together when she takes a step.

I move the wheelchair out of the way and tuck it in a corner. "You good?" I ask.

"Yes. I'm getting stronger every day. Besides, I ain't one to complain. I'm happy to be on my own two feet." She walks over to a display table selling crates of corn. She places an order, and we slowly move to the outside area.

"These peaches look delicious." I pick one up out of a box to inspect it.

"Fancy meeting you here," a familiar voice says.

I turn to see Tally. "This is a surprise." She ain't my favorite person, but I aim to be friendly while hiding my disdain.

"You took the day off?" Margret asks. I know she doesn't care for her either.

"I love this place. My parents used to come to this market a couple times a year," she says. "They have the best homemade peach ice cream." She points to a booth. "You ladies just out for the day, or are you purchasing."

Her question annoys me. "Not that it's any of your business, but we're buying for the Magnolia." So much for not showing my contempt for her.

"I love to can food." Margret tries to be sweet.

"Would you ladies like to have lunch with me?" Tally asks.

"No," I answer quickly.

"She means we've already got plans." Margret runs interference.

"Well, alright. You ladies have a good day." She glances down at Mercy. "She looks just like Ethan."

Why does every word out of her mouth make me want to yank her hair out of her head? "She does," I say with a fake grin.

She walks to another booth.

"That was fun," Margret snorts.

"Yeah, I hate her."

"Hate's a strong word." She laughs. "She does leave a bitter taste in my mouth, and I haven't even had to deal with her trying to steal my man."

"Give her time." Mercy starts to stir. She holds her hands in the air for me to pick her up.

"Hey, love bug." She snuggles into my neck. We move to the next booth, and as Margret is placing another order, I peer around, looking for Tally. She's standing near the barn talking to someone on the phone. "Oh, good, she's bothering someone else."

"What's that?" Margret asks.

"Nothing. I'm going to walk over and get some of that peach ice cream Tally mentioned. You need your wheelchair?"

"Nope. I'm good," she shoos me off.

I stand in line with Mercy by my side, holding on to my hand.

"I see you decided on the ice cream. Mercy will love it." Tally twirls a strand of my daughter's hair. "She's so darn cute."

"Look, you and I ain't friends, and I'd appreciate it if you wouldn't touch my daughter," I snap. It's one thing to mess with my husband and me, but my Mercy is off-limits.

"I was only being friendly." Her mouth gapes.

"Well, don't." I step up to the booth and order. When I turn around, Tally is nowhere in sight. "Great, maybe she'll leave us alone." I hand Mercy a small cup of ice cream, and we walk back over to Margret.

"I think I've ordered enough fruits and vegetables to get us through the winter season. And look, I found Wyatt's favorite jam." She holds up a bottle of blackberry jalapeño jam.

"He'll be happy. He eats that stuff on everything."

"Are you ready to go have lunch?"

I look down at Mercy, who is wearing more of her ice cream than she's eating. "Mercy had dessert first, but knowing her, she'll eat again." I giggle. "Let me put her back in the stroller, and I'll go get your wheelchair."

"Not necessary. I'll walk back. This has been so good for me to get out."

"Alright. I'm going to check out the booth with all the soaps before we leave. I keep an eye on Margret as she makes her way back, and I buy three bags of goat's milk soap.

She folds the walker when she's seated and hands it back to me. I put it in the backseat of the truck along with strapping Mercy in her car seat. Margret gets in, and I attach her wheelchair to the flat trailer on the back.

We drive through the small town of Farmers and find the one and only diner. It reminds me of Nita's place. We scarf down greasy hamburgers and fries. Mercy's eyes are bigger than her stomach, and she looks as if she's ready for another nap.

"Thanks for bringing me out here today. I haven't been out of Salt Lick in a long time."

"It ain't but seven miles out of town," I snort while starting up the truck.

"Still, it's good to get out. Wyatt's been struggling since Chet died. He's never been an emotional man, but his death hit him hard."

"It did all of us. I miss stomping into his house giving him a hard time about something."

"It's always amazed me at how much you are like him even though you didn't grow up in the same house. You're like Wyatt too. More so than his other siblings."

"I'll take both of those as a compliment. I feel bad for Winnie."

"Ellie says Ian has started the framework for her house on the hill next to where Chet is buried."

"You think she'll be okay up there by herself?"

"When is any Calhoun ever by themselves? Ethan will take care of his mother."

"Noah and Molly are really moving into the main house. I know that's what Daddy wanted, but it will take some getting used to."

"It will. I'm glad he left it to Noah."

"Me too." The steering wheel seems to have a

mind of its own when it pulls to one side. "What the heck?"

"I think you have a flat tire?" Margret looks out the side window.

"Great," I say, swinging open my door. Sure enough, the back passenger side tire is flat. I squat, trying to figure out if I ran over something. There's what looks like a shank on the back edge of the tire. "That's strange." As I stand, I see a black car coming up the road, slowing to pull in behind me. I walk around to the cab of the truck and take my phone out of my purse. "I'm going to call Ethan."

A man in a pair of jeans, a t-shirt, dark glasses, and a ball cap gets out of the car. He has a hand behind his back. "Looks like you ladies could use some help."

Every hair on my body rises. How did he know who was in the truck? The windows are tinted darker than they should be. I instinctively reach in to grab the pistol out of my purse.

"I wouldn't do that if I were you," the man says. The hand that was behind his back is pointing a gun directly at me.

"What do you want?" I raise my hands so he can see them.

"I want to get behind the wheel. Tell Margret to

slide over. No funny moves, or I'll kill her."

He knows our names…Rossi. I know better than to leave the site from where we are being kidnapped. "I'll go with you. Please leave them here. My daughter is in the back."

He grabs me by the hair and peers inside. He wasn't expecting her to be with us. "Keep your hands where I can see them," he tells Margret. "You get up against the truck." I don't fight him. He presses the gun in the middle of my back, then I hear him on the phone. "What the hell? You didn't mention the kid was with them. Get your ass here right now and take care of this," he seethes.

"You don't have to do this. I'll go where ever you want me to."

"Shut the hell up. Give me the keys."

"They're still in the ignition," I tell him.

"You," he says to Margret. "Open the glove box."

She does.

"Hand me the gun," he orders. He takes it from her and tucks it in his belt, all while keeping his aim on me. "Are there any other weapons?"

"No," I tell him.

"Like I'd believe you."

"Mommy," Mercy cries.

He opens the back door and shoves me inside.

"Shut her up!"

I take her out of her car seat and put her in my lap. "It's okay, ladybug."

"What do you want from us?" Margret asks.

"Payback for the trouble your husbands caused me." He looks down at Margret's legs.

"Shit! What's taking her so long?" He looks away for a split second, and I pull a small knife out from under the seat and quickly tuck it into my boot.

A silver car drives up beside us like the one Ethan described in town. I can't see who is inside because he's blocking my view. He hollers for whoever it is to get the kid.

I'm shocked when Tally gets out of the car. "You bitch!" I scream. "I knew you were up to something, and so did Ethan!"

She stands by the open door. "Give her to me." She holds out her hands.

"No!" I cry.

Rossi climbs in the front seat and leans over, with his pistol still in his hand. "You'll give her the kid, or I'll kill her. Your choice, princess."

Margret makes a move toward him and bites his arm. He yells out then backhands her in the temple. Her head bobs against the window, knocking her out cold.

"I'm going to tell you one more time. Give her the kid!"

Mercy starts to cry. "It's okay, baby. She's not going to hurt you because if she does, your daddy will hunt her to the end of the earth and kill her." I don't want to give her to Tally, but it's the only way I can keep her safe from Rossi. I don't know if he's capable of murdering an innocent child or not. Tally may be a total bitch, but there's no way she'd hurt her.

Mercy cries harder when Tally takes her from me. I reach around the front to check a pulse on Margret. "She needs a doctor."

"She'll survive." With one hand, he goes through her purse, taking her phone. "Give me your cell phone," he barks.

I pick up my purse to give it to him and remember I took my old phone back from Ethan so I could donate it. I fish out the old one, handing it to him, and when he looks away, I stick the new one in Mercy's bag. Ethan told me he has a tracker on it. "Please give her my daughter's bag. She'll need water and snacks." I hold it up.

"Get out!" He snatches it from me, tossing it to Tally.

Sliding out, I check my surroundings to see if there are any cars coming. Nothing but empty road.

"Get behind the wheel of my car." He shoves me hard.

I climb inside, and as he's walking to the other side, I slide my hand to my boot, pulling out the knife, keeping a firm grip on the handle. The door opens, and he leans down to get in. When he does, I stab the blade in his side. He yells out in pain but doesn't release his gun. With blood oozing from his side, he yanks the knife out, tossing it out the window, then grasps my hair, shoving me in the seat. "I should kill you. You're lucky I want to make your husband suffer." With his blood smeared on my face, he pushes me upright. "Drive," he says, pointing the gun at me with one hand; the other is applying pressure to his side.

"Where are we going?" I ask, driving out onto the road. Margret is still against the window, and Tally has taken out Mercy's car seat and is putting it in her vehicle.

"You'll find out when we get there," he grits.

"You know this isn't going to end well for you. When Ethan finds out what you've done, he'll kill you."

"You seem to forget, I'm the one in control. Once

I'm done with Ethan, he'll regret the day he ever laid eyes on me."

"You're sick," I spit out.

"And, you are much prettier than your pictures. I bet you're one hot little number in the sack. No wonder Ethan waited on you to come back. I may have to taint his beautiful bride."

His gaze sickeningly roams my body, bringing bile into my throat. I breathe in deep and blow out, trying not to lose my lunch. "What did you promise Tally to get her to do your dirty work?"

"It didn't take much convincing. With you out of the picture for good, she'll consult your husband. She'll be a hero for rescuing your daughter. That wasn't in my plan, but it'll be an edge for her."

Despair starts to gnaw in my gut. "Where is she taking her?"

"I have no idea. I'm sure she's going to wing it."

"What about Margret?"

"I was going to make Wyatt suffer too. I don't have time for a cripple. She's lucky, or she'd have the same fate as you."

My heart kicks a ruckus in my chest, mingling with fear. I'm on my own. No one is going to save me. I have to keep a clear head. Ethan will find Mercy, and Margret will get help.

"*D*amn you, Bellamy!" I yell into my phone. "I told you Rose would never sell the vineyard. Why the hell did you come here?"

"You failed for the first time since I've known you, so I considered it a personal challenge to prove you wrong. I thought maybe you were playing her. I can see that you weren't. You really love the country girl, don't you?"

"She's more woman than anyone I've ever met."

"I guess I misjudged you when I hired you. I thought you left the country for good. I did my best to hide it from everyone."

"The country has never been out of me, nor do I want it to be. I despise the way I used women for the all-loving dollar."

"You're a rich man because of me."

"I'd rather be dirt poor."

"Ah, but you'll go to bed tonight knowing that you're not." He laughs. "That lass is going to buy you nothing but trouble and heartache. She's a wild one."

"You don't know her like I do," I growl.

"I'm not giving up on buying her gold mine. I'll keep sending her offers until she caves."

"She won't. Money doesn't mean anything to Rose."

"If money means nothing to her, then why does she do what she does? For the pure please of making wine? No, everyone can be bought."

"Not Rose."

"For your sake, I hope I'm wrong. If you ever want your job back, you can beg me for it. In the end, I'll hire you because you're good at what you do."

"Thanks, but no thanks. I'm going to enjoy being a rancher."

"Suit yourself."

Driving back to the bed-and-breakfast, I'm surprised when I see Molly Calhoun at the guest desk. "Hi, Molly."

"Hey," she says, looking up from the computer.

"Where's Jane?"

CHAPTER TWENTY ONE

"She and Margret took off for the day. Nita and I are covering for them."

"Good thing I ran into you. I was going to give you a call and see if I could meet with you about buying a house with property?"

"You're moving here? I thought you loved California."

"When you fall in love with a feisty redhead, things change."

Her eyes fly open wide. "You and Rose?"

"She doesn't realize she loves me yet, but she will."

"You have your work cut out for you. Rose is all business."

"She has a soft side when you get her to let her guard down."

She rests her elbows on the counter, placing her chin on her knuckles. "Tucker's told me many times you're a confirmed lifetime bachelor."

"I thought I would be. Rose is different."

"Sounds like you're a man in love. I've got the perfect piece of property that hasn't even gone on the market yet. It's not far from the vineyard. It's a twenty-acre plot with a large house. It needs some remodeling. It's a four-bedroom with an office."

"Too big for what we need, but I guess instead of

remodeling it, I could tear it down and build a smaller home."

"You don't want room to grow?" She waggles her eyebrows.

"No. Neither one of us want kids. Nieces and nephews will be more than enough. I think Tucker and Missy are planning to repopulate the Earth." I chuckle.

"I can show you the place tomorrow."

"That would be great." I slap the palm of my hand on the counter. "There is one other thing I'd like to arrange after I purchase a house."

"What's that?"

"I'd like to donate a large sum of money."

"Do you have a specific cause in mind?"

"I do, but we can discuss the details later." I head up the stairs to my room. I notice the door is ajar. Slowly opening it, I see Rose sitting on my couch. "How did you get in here without anyone seeing you?" I close the door.

"I came up the back entrance."

"And you broke into my room?" I sit beside her.

She holds out her wrists. "You can have me arrested if you'd like."

I'd love nothing more than to cuff her myself and

watch her squirm. I brush a tendril of hair behind her ear. "Are you here to tell me you love me?"

"Sort of?" She shifts her body toward me.

"I'm listening."

"Did you mean what you said?"

"I said a lot of things. You're going to have to be more specific." I angle my head to lock eyes with her.

"That you would love me even if I have cancer?"

"Absolutely. It would not change a thing."

"But, if I lose my teeth…you're out." The corners of her lips turn upward.

"I draw the line at no teeth." I take my finger and draw a line between the two of us.

She stands. "Do you want to touch them?"

I lift my chin to look at her. "Your teeth?"

She laughs, and it's a beautiful thing. "No, silly, my breasts."

I stand. "You never have to ask me if I want to touch your breasts."

"What if there is nothing but an ugly scar in their place?"

"I'll kiss the scars to show you how much I love you."

"Then my hot minute is up." She places her hand on the side of my face.

"What are you saying, Rose." My chest rises with hope.

"I'm saying, I love you. I don't know how it's going to work between us. I only know that I want to try."

Raising my hand, I place it under her hair on the back of her neck. "I've quit my job, and I'm going to buy a place for us to live when you're ready to marry me." Her eyes are frozen with mine, and we're mere inches apart.

"Do you want to marry me?" Her breath has changed to small pants of air.

"More than anything in the world. I've never felt this way about another human being, and I'm not willing to let go of this feeling, Rose. I know it's a corny line, but you really do complete me. I had no idea what I was missing until the day I stepped onto the deck of the vineyard."

"I loved that you quoted Shakespeare."

"You are my Rose." She rises up on her toes and kisses me. As she does, she lifts my hand to her chest.

She needs this; she needs me to touch her. Sweeping the blouse from her shoulder, I lean down, placing my lips on her clavicle and cupping her breast. "You are so damn beautiful." My hand slides over her heart. "This is all I need from you."

A single tear slides down from the corner of her eye to her cheek. "I love you, Dodge."

I lift her in my arms, carting her to the bed. She undresses before I get the chance to, then she unbuckles my belt. Laying her back on the bed, I cover her body with mine, kissing her, then moving to her nipples. She hisses, and her body starts to shiver. I lift my gaze to try to gauge what she's feeling. She smiles, letting me know she wants more. Standing, I strip out of my clothes then sit on the side of the bed. Drawing her hand into mine, I tug her to me, and she straddles my lap. Her breasts are in the perfect spot. Her legs clasp around me tight when I suck and bite at her nipples.

"Yes," she hisses.

I take my time driving her crazy before I flip her onto her back. Her hands find their way between us, and she strokes me. "I've never gotten a good look at you up close before," she says.

"And?" I cock my head.

"You're gorgeous." Her gaze inches downward. "Every inch of you."

"I'm glad you're enjoying the view." I chuckle.

"You have a nice ass too." She giggles and slaps my butt cheek.

"Be careful. Turnabout is fair play."

Her cheeks darken. "You want to spank me?"

"Not today. But one day, I will." I can't stand not being inside her for one second longer. I raise up between her legs and position myself at her core. She lifts her head, watching me slowly sink into her. She bites her lip, holding back a moan. It's so erotic to me. I've never actually made love to a woman, only quick dirty sex. The look on her face hits me in the heart, spurring on my desire for her. I have no control of my body anymore. I move hard; she does the same. Her nails dig into my back, covered in a fine mist of sweat. I'm completely lost in her and she in me.

I pull out, wanting a taste of her. My head dips between her thighs, and her entire body goes rigid. "It's okay, Rose. Trust me."

She shakes her head, and I slide my tongue into her. After a few swipes, her body relaxes, and she puts her hands on my head. No one has ever taken the time to really love her. I plan on not letting her forget where I've been.

She lets out a scream and comes in my mouth. When she's done, I delve deep into her, clutching her ass and rocking her hips. She builds quickly again and clenches down around my cock. I try to hold on but can't. Arching back, I groan as I thrust deeper, letting go.

I prop up over her, bracing my elbows on the bed. Our chests are rising and falling in tandem.

"That was fantastic," she says breathlessly.

"Thank you for trusting me," I say, staring into her eyes. "Thank you for letting me be the one to truly make love to you."

She licks her lips. "You're more than welcome." She's wearing a silly grin. "The pleasure was all mine."

I glance between us. "Um…I think I shared in some of it."

She jerks my head up playfully by my hair. "We can do that again anytime you're ready."

I roll off of her onto my back. "To coin your phrase, you may have to give me a hot minute."

She bursts out laughing, laying her head on my shoulder. "I'm glad I snuck over."

"Me too."

"I promised my employee I wouldn't be gone long if she'd cover for me, so I really do need to go."

"How about if I stay at your place tonight? I have a few errands to run."

She crawls out of bed to get dressed. "I'll cook

dinner, and we can share a glass or two of Boone's Brand."

I skirt up onto my elbows to watch her. "Sounds good."

She walks over to the closet, opening it. Pushing a few hangers to the side, she finds what she's looking for. "I love this blue plaid shirt on you."

"I'll never wear another shirt," I tease.

"These suits, not so much, but this one"—she holds up a gray sports coat—"I like."

"Do I get to go through your closet and tell you what I like and don't like?" I chuckle.

"If you'd like."

"Good, get rid of everything. I want you completely naked."

"It might bring in more male patrons." She bats her eyes.

"Never mind. I don't want to have to kill a man for looking at you." I scoot to a sitting position in the middle of the bed, folding my hands behind my head.

She walks over, planting a kiss on my shoulder. "You have nothing to be worried about. I will see you later."

"Thanks for breaking and entering." I smile.

She blows me a kiss, walking out.

My heart is completely full. Seven weeks ago, when I arrived here, never in a million years did I think I'd fall head over heels in love. That ache for her has always been there, but I was strong enough to walk away. I'm glad I finally gave into it. I feel free for the first time in my life. I'm no longer worried about becoming my father. I'm my own man, and this man only wants Rose. I'd say she's changed me. Yet, I've always been this man underneath dying to get out. Rose helped release him.

CHAPTER TWENTY TWO

ETHAN

"Have you heard from your wife? I haven't been able to get ahold of Margret for hours now," Wyatt says, marching into my office.

I glance at my watch. "No. She told me they wouldn't be home until mid-day. What are you doing in town?"

"I met Noah at the bank to finalize Dad's will on the property." He walks over to my window in my office, looking out.

"How are you doing?" He's struggling with Chet's death.

"I never thought I'd miss the old man as much as I do." He doesn't turn around.

"His loss has most assuredly left a hole in our hearts."

"There isn't a place in this town that doesn't remind me of him."

"Clem thinks we should have dinner every Sunday at the main house in his honor."

He peers over his shoulder. "What do Noah and Molly think about that idea?"

"Clem said they were all on board."

He ambles toward my desk. "How is Winnie?"

"She's staying busy at the pet store. When she's not working, she's spending time with all the grandkids."

"I know. I appreciate her taking our kids today so Margret could get away." He takes out his phone as if he's wishing for it to ring.

"You're worried," I state.

"It's just not like her to not touch base with me."

"I'll try Jane's phone." I bring up her number and hit the button. "That's odd," I frown. "It went straight to voicemail." I switch over to the locator to find her. "This shows her on the road from Farmers. They probably don't have a signal. I'm sure they'll be home soon."

He scratches his head. "You're right. I'm worrying for nothing."

My phone vibrates on my desk. "It's Jane's old number," I mutter before I pick it up. "Wyatt and I were just talking about the two of you. Why aren't you using your new phone?"

"Ethan, I'm leaving town. The stress of losing my father is too much."

I sit tall. "Jane, where are you? We can talk about this."

"There's nothing to talk about. I'm closing out the account my father left for me, but the bank is saying Wyatt has to okay it."

I put her on speakerphone. "Wyatt happens to be right here? What's the location of the bank you're at right now?"

"Everything can be done by phone."

"Jane, where's Mercy and Margret?" Fear is boiling in my gut.

"Mercy's in good hands. Margret should be home shortly."

"What do you mean Mercy is in good hands. Where the hell is she?" I'm on my feet.

"Ethan, please put Wyatt on the phone."

"Don't do this, Jane. I can take you to the counselor, and we can work through what you're feeling together."

"I can't, Ethan. I need to get away."

"If you do this, there's no coming back. How

could you do this to your daughter?" That same fear in my gut is prickling my scalp.

"She'll be better off without me."

A hitch in her voice tells me she's not doing this on her own accord. Wyatt and I share an understanding look.

"I'm right here, Jane. Put the bank manager on the phone," he tells her.

She does, and Wyatt okays the money to be released. "I'll have it ready for her shortly," he says.

"Put Jane back on the phone," I bark harshly.

"Ethan, I'm sorry," she says.

"Does Rossi have you?" I question softly.

"I gotta go. Please forgive me. I told you I'd never leave you again." The line goes dead.

"Jane! Jane! Damn it! Rossi has her. Where the hell is my daughter?" I look at the tracker again.

Wyatt's phone rings. "I can't talk right now, Dodge…" He stops speaking.

"I found Margret slumped over in Jane's truck outside of Farmers. I was running an errand and saw the truck on the side of the road with a flat tire."

His jaw clenches. "Is she okay?"

"She took a good hit to the side of the head. She's awake now but out of sorts."

"Is Mercy with her?"

I hear him ask her about Mercy. "She says Tally took her."

"Tally?" I barrel out of my office to hers. "Where is she?" I yell at her secretary.

"She took the day off?" She's confused by my anger.

"Get her on the phone right now!"

She calls her. "There's no answer."

I growl and find Wyatt standing behind me. "I've told Dodge not to move her. I'm going to where she is, and on my way, I'm calling Mike."

"I'll be right behind you." I turn to the secretary. "If she calls back, find out where she is." As I'm storming behind Wyatt down the stairs three at a time, something hits me, stopping me dead in my tracks.

Wyatt looks over the rail at me. "Why'd you stop?"

"The phone. Jane called me on her old one, so my phone is tracking someone. If Margret is still, then Jane must've put the phone in Mercy's bag."

"Smart girl," Wyatt says, and we bolt down the steps. "I'll go to Margret. You follow the signal. Once I know Margret is safe, I'll call you. I'll tell Mike what's happened."

I grab his elbow. "I want to find Jane without the help of the police."

He nods with understanding knowing I'll take Rossi out. "Call Boone, get him to help you. You're gonna need back up."

Ripping the door of my truck open, the engine fires up as I turn the key. I place my phone in the holder so I can follow the map. As soon as I'm moving, I call Boone.

"I need your help," I say before he can respond. "Rossi has Jane, and Tally has Mercy. I'm following the tracking signal on Jane's phone. I believe it will lead me to Tally."

"Damn. Where do you want me to meet you?"

I scroll through the signal. "She can't be that stupid? It's taking me to her house."

"I'm on my way," he says, without hesitation.

"Don't pull in her driveway. I don't want her to see us coming. I may have to play her game to find out where Rossi is taking Jane. Go through the back but keep out of sight."

"We'll get them both back," he says before he hangs up.

I drive like a demon to Tally's, slowing when I enter the driveway. When I park, I lean over the back seat, picking up a file. There's nothing important in it, but I need an excuse to be here. Boone texts me, letting me know he's in place. Reaching in the center console, I take out my gun, put in the clip, and place it in my shoulder holster. Tally is used to seeing me carry it outside of work.

I take a big inhale, calming my fears before stepping out of my truck. I ring the doorbell and wait. Tally peeks out a side window then comes to the door, opening it slightly.

"Ethan!" She rushes to open the door. "I'm so glad you're here." She throws herself in my arms.

I pull her off me and walk into her house, scoping the place out. Tally's white blouse is ripped, and her hair is a mess. "What happened?"

"It's Rossi. I happened to be in Farmers the same time as Jane and Margret. I saw them on the side of the road and stopped to help. Rossi was holding them at gunpoint. I convinced him to let me take Mercy after he roughed me up a bit." Her eyes fill with fake tears.

"Where is she?" I growl

"She's upstairs sleeping. Poor thing was traumatized."

"Why didn't you call me right away or call the police?"

Her hands flitter in the air. "I don't know. I think

I was in shock. I wanted to get Mercy safe before I did anything else."

"Where did he take Jane and Margret?"

"I…I don't know," she cries. "Please hold me. I'm so frightened."

"I need you to think, Tally. Did he say anything?"

"No," she sobs. "Why would he tell me anything?"

As if on cue, Boone walks in, bracing his rifle on his shoulder. "Because you helped him orchestrate kidnapping Jane."

Tally flinches. "That's not true. I saved your daughter."

"Did you really think when Margret came to, she wouldn't tell us your involvement."

"He was supposed to take care of her." She covers her mouth with her hand.

"I guess he left a loose end for you to get caught."

"That bastard!"

She tries to run away, but I snatch her arm. "You aren't going anywhere but to jail. What did you really think you were going to gain from working with Rossi?"

"You!" she yells. "I was finally going to get you!" she bellows. "You'd be devastated Jane left you again, and I saved your only child. I could give you more." She touches my cheek, and my skin crawls.

CHAPTER TWENTY TWO

"You're sicker than he is."

"Don't say that!" She slaps me across the face.

"I've never struck a woman in anger in all my life, but you're pushing me, Tally. You're going to take me to my daughter!"

Boone walks over, shoving the rifle in her back. "Move." His tone is menacing even to me.

We follow her upstairs to a room at the end of the hall. She pushes it open and steps out of the way. Mercy stirs when I walk in.

"Daddeee," she squeals. Tears sit heavy on the bottom of her eyelids.

"Daddy's got you," I say, clutching her to my chest.

"Where's Mommy?" she whines.

"I'm going to find her. Don't you worry, love bug." I turn toward Tally. "If you would've harmed her in any way, you'd have been taken out of here in a body bag."

"I would never hurt a child." She wrenches her arms across her chest.

"You need to start talking. How and when did Rossi contact you," Boone questions.

"It was a couple weeks ago. He called my office. At first, it frightened me. The more he spoke, I realized by what he wanted, I could finally get what I deserved."

"You're gonna get what you deserve, alright," Boone hisses.

"You set them up?" I seethe.

"All I had to do was find a time when the two of them would be together and out of your reach."

"So, you followed them today and let Rossi know their every move." It's a statement, not a question. "Where did he take Jane?"

"I don't know."

"He had to have said something!" I roar, startling Mercy. She cries. "Daddy's sorry." I hold her tighter. "I need to get her somewhere safe, and then you're going to go over every word Rossi has ever said to you."

"I have rope in the back of my truck. I'll tie her up." Boone smirks at her.

Her eyes widen. "Aren't you going to call the police?"

"No," I snap.

"I'd rather deal with the police than him." She indicates Boone with a shift of her head.

"Too bad. We're handling this my way." Boone directs her down the stairs with his rifle still perched on his shoulder. "Don't even think about making a run for it. I won't miss."

I tie her hands while Boone keeps his aim. Mercy clings onto my legs. I hate that she has to see any of this and hope it won't scar her for life.

"Tally comes with me. Take Mercy to Clem. I'll meet you in the run-down barn at the back of the property."

I fasten Mercy in her seat and call Wyatt. "How is Margret?"

"I'm taking her to Doc's to get her checked out. The bastard hit her in the side of the head after she took a chunk out of him with her teeth. Did you find Mercy?"

"Yes, she's safe. Tally had her. She worked with Rossi to make all this happen. Boone has her tied up and is going to question her to see what else she knows."

"What was her motive?"

"Me. She thought I'd fall for her if Jane was permanently out of the picture. She tried to convince me she saved Mercy from him."

"Damn."

"I have no doubt, Boone will break her if she knows anything."

"Dodge is headed to the main house. I'll meet you once I know Margret is okay. Nita is going to take her home."

"I appreciate the help, but I don't want anyone else involved. Alert Bear, Ian, and Noah so they can keep an eye out at the ranch."

"Whatever you do, I'm going with you. Rossi was after my wife too."

"I don't think I could stop you even if I wanted to."

CHAPTER TWENTY THREE

JANE

"I've done everything you've asked. Now let me go!" I try to break away from his grasp, but it's no use. He clamps down harder on my arm.

"I've only just begun to torture your husband," he snarls, shoving me in the passenger's side the sliding in next to me. His weapon is pressing into my ribs.

"You know the bank manager is going to call the police."

"Let him. We'll be long gone. Now drive!"

I pull out into traffic.

"Make a right." He points.

I do as he says.

"The alley." He motions to the left. "Pull up beside the delivery truck."

When I park, he pulls the keys from the ignition and reaches behind him for a black bag. "Hold your hands out," he orders.

I don't do it, and he yanks my hair hard. I cry out, and he pulls harder.

"Shut the hell up." When he has me pinned in his lap, he zip-ties my hands together then shoves me to a sitting position. "I don't want any trouble out of you."

He gets out of the car and is met by a man coming out of a door in the alley. I can't hear what they're saying. Rossi hands him an envelope in exchange for keys. As they're talking, I flip open the door and take off running for my life.

"Help me!" I scream. A car darts in front of me, and I roll over the hood, landing hard on my knee. Screaming out in pain, my mouth is covered when Rossi is on top of me.

"You bitch!" he yells when I bite his hand. The butt of his gun crashes on my cheek. The pain is so sharp I can't move. Rossi waves the driver off with his gun.

Dragging me off the ground, he tosses me like a sack of potatoes into the back of the delivery truck. Before he shuts the door, I see the other man take off in Rossi's car.

"On second thought," he says. "I don't trust you." He climbs in and digs through a bag the man had stashed and takes out a rope. He binds it around my waist then ties it to a metal loop on the wall. He tugs hard, making sure I can't get free.

Raising my shoulder, I wipe the blood on my face. It hurts, but not as bad as my knee. My jeans are torn, and I can see redness and swelling have already started. "I'm hurt," I cry when he climbs behind the wheel. "I need a doctor."

"No doctor." He shoves the truck in reverse, then takes off so fast it slams me against the frame. My eyesight blurs, and everything goes dark.

***

"WAKE UP!" I hear and try to open my eyes.

My left eye is almost swollen shut, and when I move, pain spears through my leg.

"Get up!" Rossi growls.

"I can't." My voice is faint.

He climbs in, hauling me to my feet. I can't put weight on my leg. He leans me against the side of the door then unties my waist. Then he throws me over his shoulder. When he jumps down, his shoulder digs into my stomach.

"Please stop," I cry.

He doesn't slow his movement. Lifting my head, I look at my surroundings. We're in the woods with no one in sight. Rossi kicks open the door to a cabin and sets me on the couch.

"Please take this off. I can't walk to go anywhere." I hold out my hands.

He pulls a knife from his boot and cuts my binds off. Ripping off his shirt scares me. I attempt to scream, but my throat seizes up. Not that it would do any good; there's no one here but us.

"You are going to stitch up the hole you put in my side." He disappears and comes back with a medical kit.

"Why would I help you?" I snarl.

"Because if you don't, you'll die out here alone."

"Isn't your plan to kill me anyway?"

"You seem to forget, with one phone call, I could have your daughter killed."

I swallow hard. "I'll need to clean the wound first."

"That's what I thought." He's so smug. Laying down on the couch, he keeps his gun clutched in his hand. "I'm watching every move you make."

I gingerly slide myself to the floor, being careful of my knee. Opening the kit, I take out alcohol and sutures. There is a surgical blade in the box. He is prepped for all kinds of emergencies. I hold up a vial. "Do you want me to give you lidocaine?"

"No. I don't trust you with the needle."

"Suit yourself. It's gonna hurt."

Ripping the package of gauze, I douse it with alcohol and clean the wound. He hisses a few times but never takes his stare off me. Once I'm done, I pull the hooped needle from the suture kit. My hand shakes as I stick it through one side of the wound, then the other. He tights his rib cage with every tug of the suture. When I'm done, I tie it off and clip the needle, setting it slowly on the table.

He sits, glancing down at my handiwork. "Not bad."

"I've sewn a few animals in my day."

"Part of being a rancher's wife." He glares at me for a moment with hardness, then it softens. "Let me help you on the couch. You look like you could use a bit of medical care yourself.

I don't fight him when he lifts me under the arms, placing me on the couch. Ripping open a gauze and opening a pink plastic vile of saline, he pours it on the gauze. He lays his gun on his lap, lifts my chin with a knuckle, then gently cleans my cheek and around my eye.

"I can see why Ethan loves you so much," he says. "Even with your eye swollen shut, you're a beautiful woman and feisty as hell."

"Have you ever been married?" I decide to take advantage of his softer moment.

"No. A life of crime isn't suitable for a woman."

"You're a smart man. You could give it up."

"And do what?" He laughs. "Work a nine to five job and be a slave to the man?"

"There are plenty of things you could do and be your own boss."

"This is what I was born to do. I'm good at it."

"Kidnapping women?"

He hangs his head. "No, this is the down part to the job." His head rises, and I see the evil in him return. "Your husband has to pay for what he cost me."

"I gave you all the money I had."

"It's not about money. It's about respect."

"Respect for a criminal?"

He stands. "That may be how you see me. I'm a man making a living and providing a good one for the men who work for me." He shrugs on his shirt.

Stay here. I'll be right back. He picks up the medical kit and walks out the front door.

He sees himself as a good guy. An entrepreneur. He's twisted. Bracing my hands on the seat, I try to stand. It's no use. I can't straighten my leg to put any weight on it. I need to try and find out where he brought me. Will Ethan be able to find me? I have to get out of here.

The door opens, and he comes in with two pieces of wood and bindings.

"You don't have to tie me down. I can't run away."

He doesn't say anything. He lays the wood on the table and then gently lifts both my legs on the couch. "I don't want to have to carry you everywhere," he says, bracing the wood on either side of my injured leg. He wraps the rope around it, securing the wood. "There are crutches in the closet." He stands.

"You're very prepared."

He opens the closet and hands them to me. "You'll have to adjust them."

"Thank you," I say, taking them from him. "Where are we?"

"Far enough out that no one can find you."

He opens what looks like a well-stocked refrigerator and tosses me a bottle of water. "Drink," he barks.

The cool water eases the dryness of my throat. Tears rain down as I think about Ethan. I hate what I said to him. Rossi knew well enough that me telling him I was leaving would be the one thing that would destroy Ethan. "I'd never leave you," I whisper to myself, "nor our daughter." Mercy...I pray Tally didn't hurt her.

"Are you hungry?"

"No."

"You need to eat. That leg won't heal if you don't," he tosses me a protein bar.

"What I need is to go to the hospital."

"That's not happening," he says.

"What's next on your agenda? Are you waiting for Ethan to find you?"

"He won't. No one knows about this place." He walks over to me. "Give me your wedding ring?"

"What? No?" I slide my hand under my thigh.

"You can either give it to me, or I'll cut your finger off." He holds his hand out.

"What are you going to do with it," I ask, giving him my wedding band.

"Torture your husband." He takes out his cell phone and tugs my head back by the hair again, and snaps a picture. "This should piss him off." He taps his phone. I can only assume he sent the photo to Ethan.

"In your sick twisted mind, you think you're the good guy and Ethan is bad. There is no better man than my husband, and the good guys always win. He will find you and kill you."

"Perhaps, but they'll be nothing left of his family when I'm done with him. Now, be a good girl while I get a hot shower." He disappears into another room.

I brace myself on my crutches and open the front door. There are trees as far as I can see. Making my way over to the delivery truck, I peer inside for the keys. No such luck. I could walk out into the woods, but I have no idea which direction to go. I'd get lost and die out there. There's a shed behind the house, but even from here, I can see a padlock.

Going back to the house, I reside myself to staying put for now. At some point, he has to sleep. I'll get his phone and keys and make my escape. Settling back on the couch, I lay down, tucking a pillow over my head. If I'm going to get away at night, I need to take advantage of sleeping while I can. Closing my eyes, my mind reels. Ethan has to be beside himself. Will he even bother looking for me after I told him I was leaving. He's a smart man. He'll figure it out. By now, he's tracked Mercy. God, I pray she's safely in his arms. Rossi didn't kill Margret. She'll wake up and tell them about Tally if she didn't kill her. She's a lot of things, but I don't believe she would take someone's life.

Then my thoughts run to my father. If he weren't dead, this would surely kill him. I miss him so much. I could always count on him for a swift kick in the ass, followed by unconditional love. What I'd give to see him burst through the door on Ethan's heels. I don't know who would take him out first. I need to think more like them. What would they do in this situation? They'd be mindful of everything around them. Keep their eyes open.

I reach over and grab the protein bar Rossi gave me. I have to keep my strength up. That would be the first thing Ethan would say. I can't outsmart him if I have no fuel.

Finishing the bar, I curl up, wincing when I try to move my leg. Ignoring the pain, I drift off to sleep.

"*I*'m going with you," Dodge says, tagging along behind me as I open the barn door.

"Why is he here?" Boone barks.

"He followed me." I walk over to the old stall, dragging the door open to see Tally still tied up, lying against the wall.

"Thank God you're here. This bully manhandled me," she spats.

"I like how you think I'm going to save you," I sneer.

"I want to help," Dodge tells Boone.

"You need to stay behind and take care of my daughter."

"She's safe where she is. I sent her over to the

bed-and-breakfast. Ian is taking care of her, Molly, and Nita. Bear and Noah have everyone else on lockdown at the main house."

"That's not good enough. Go help Ian at the Magnolia. I'm not going to be responsible for anything happening to you," Boone braces his hand on his shoulder.

"He's right," Wyatt says, in the door.

"I appreciate you want to help, but I can't risk another person and the choice that will be made once we find Rossi."

"I can handle it," he retorts. "I know my way around a gun. I know you think I'm more of a city boy, but I'm not. I can hunt with the best of them."

"The answer is no," Boone growls. "The only thing you need to worry about is taking care of my daughter. If any harm comes to her, I'll hold you responsible." He points at Dodge.

"Yes, sir," he finally relents. "Can I at least help you brainstorm where to find her?"

"Fine. Then your ass is out of here," Boone states.

I walk into where Tally is and squat in front of her. "Tell me what you know."

"I've already told grape ape over there. I don't have any idea where he took her," she snarls at Boone.

Boone kicks the boot of his toe in the dirt, spits, then walks over to her with his rifle gripped in his hand. "You know there are bodies buried here no one knows about. You can join them if you like."

She squeezes her eyes tight. "He told me he wanted to take Jane to make you pay."

My phone dings in my pocket. I pull it out and see the face of my wife. Her eye is swollen shut, and she has a deep gash on her cheek. "Damn it!" I yell.

"What is it?" Wyatt asks. I show him the picture.

"I will end his life," I spit out.

Taking both hands, I grab Tally by the collar. "Where the hell did he take her?"

"Is there anything in the picture that might give away his location?" Dodge takes my phone and zooms out. "From the looks of it, it's a cabin."

"Did he own a cabin?" I yell at Tally.

"I don't recall. You read as many reports on him as I did," she starts to cry.

I get up and pace, trying to visualize everything I researched on him. "He didn't own anything, so he couldn't be tracked."

"How about a family member, maybe a parent?" Dodge says.

"That's it." I snap my fingers. "One of the reports stated his father used to own a cabin in Tennessee. It was an off-the-grid kinda place, so there was no exact location on it. I remember Mike trying to locate it when we were searching for him. He couldn't even pinpoint it. When Rossi was arrested, he told him the place had burnt down years ago."

"Like he could be trusted," Wyatt says.

"Rossi mentioned Tennessee in one of our conversations," Tally pipes in. "He said people could get lost in that state."

"That has to be it." Boone shuffles over to Wyatt. "Call your contact in the land department, see what he can come up with."

"If Mike couldn't locate it, I'm not sure the land department can."

Dodge gets on his phone. "Hey Molly, can you access land maps in Tennessee. Off-grid type locations," he asks her, then listens.

"Not a bad idea." Wyatt nudges Boone.

"Are you going to untie me now," Tally whines.

"You'll get untied when I haul your ass to jail." I tug at her binds.

"What are we going to do with her in the meantime?" Wyatt looks down at her.

"We can lock her in the storm shelter. When this is all over, Mike can send his men for her."

"No," she gasps. "Please, I helped you."

"You set up my wife to be kidnapped. Not to mention Margret and Mercy! There is no way you're going free." My voice booms through the thin walls of the barn.

"I told Molly about Rossi's father. She found an old record of land owned by a man with the same last name. It says the owner is deceased. The property was left to his heir, but names are not printed on the deed. She's sending the information to your phone." Dodge ends his conversation with Molly.

My phone beeps again. I study the map. "This is only three hours from here." I glance at my watch. "He's had plenty of time to make it there based on the time the bank manager said they left."

"This is the only thing we have to go on. It's a long shot, but we better get moving." Boone grasps Tally by the arm, helping her off the ground. "I'll take care of her. Come with me," he tells Dodge.

"Thanks for your help, Dodge. You may have saved my wife's life if your information is correct."

He nods, following Boone out."

"We need ammo. Handguns would be best. Boone's rifle will be good to scope out the area first. I'll grab a first aid kit from my truck in case we need it." Wyatt is processing our needs.

"We'll take my truck. I have blankets and a first

aid kit already stocked. It will be dark by the time we get there. The element of surprise may work in our favor."

Wyatt scratches his head. "I hope we have the right location."

"I'm counting on it."

"I'm going to call the Magnolia, make sure everything is okay." Wyatt pulls out his phone and heads outside with me on his heels.

"I'm going to call my mother. I know how worried she is." I call, and there is no answer. I try Clem's phone. "Hey, is my mother there with you?"

"No. That last time I spoke with her, she was locking up the pet store and headed home."

"I thought she was watching the kids? When was that?"

"A couple of hours ago. Ellie said when she came over to help with the kids, Winnie needed to run to the store. She had someone buying a puppy. This was before we knew anything about Jane missing. Maybe she went to the Magnolia."

"No, I specifically told her to come straight home," I growl. "Call me if she shows up." I snag Wyatt on the way to my truck.

"What else has happened?"

"My mother is missing."

CHAPTER TWENTY FOUR

"You think Rossi has her?"

"I don't know." I haul ass through the grass and over the hills, only stopping to pick up Boone. "Get in!" I yell.

He locks the storm shelter and hops in the backseat. "She's contained, and Dodge is on his way to Rose."

"Winnie never made it to the main house," Wyatt tells him.

"Fuck!" Boone beats the back of the seat.

My truck nearly goes on two wheels on I turn off Whiskey River onto the main road. Zooming down the highway, I don't brake until we're in front of my mother's shop. The truck barely stops rolling when I jump out. The closed sign is flipped over. I beat on the door. "Mother!" I yell.

Wyatt tries the window.

I run around to the back entrance and find the door wide open. Boxes are toppled over, and her purse is perched on the floor. Boone storms in behind me, scanning the store.

"This looks like the only sign of a struggle. There's no blood anywhere."

"Rossi can't be in two places at one time. My bet is on the guy that was following me and that Tally was talking to in the care that day outside the diner."

We load in my truck and stop at the gun store to load up on ammo and purchase bulletproof vests for each of us. "Do you have a map of Tennessee?" I ask the owner.

He flips through a few maps behind the counter and pulls one out. "There's great hunting up there," he says, handing it to me.

I pay him, and we're out the door. Boone tosses water bottles over the seat. "Drink. We're going to need to stay hydrated."

Wyatt downs the bottle of water then tilts his hat downward to cover his eyes. "I'm going to try to get a few minutes of shut-eye while I can."

It isn't long, and he's out.

In the rearview mirror, I can see Boone gnawing on the inside of his cheek. His elbow is propped on the window and his dark glasses keep me from seeing his eyes, but it's obvious he's brewing.

"Do you have a plan," I ask him.

"I've been studying this map. There's an old fire tower up the hill from where Molly indicated a house to be. I think we should start there. I can scope it out with binoculars. It might be within good shooting range too."

"I want to be the one to take him out."

"I'll let you handle it unless you can't."

"Jane's safety and my mother's is my first priority. Once I know they are safe, Rossi is all mine."

***

THREE HOURS LATER, we're at the fire tower. "It's too dark to see anything."

Boone takes out his binoculars anyway. "Too bad we didn't snag a pair of night goggles."

"Speak for yourself." Wyatt pulls a pair out of his bag. "I saw them when we were in the gun shop. I figured they might come in handy." He hands them to Boone.

"Thanks, man." I clap his shoulder.

"I see a cabin a half mile in. There's a delivery truck parked out back."

"How the hell did a delivery truck find this place?" Wyatt asks.

"Are there any lights on?"

"There's one light coming from a side window. If it weren't for being lit, I wouldn't have seen the cabin."

"Any movement?" I question.

"No."

"We might have to wait until morning." Wyatt takes blankets from his bag. "I'll keep first watch. You two get some shut-eye."

"I won't be able to sleep," I tell him.

Boone hands Wyatt the rifle and the night goggles. "Wake me if anything stirs." He lays down, bunching up the blanket under his head.

"I'm sorry, man. I never asked you any more about Margret."

"You've been a little preoccupied. She's going to have a headache, but other than that, Doc says she's fine. She's pissed off yet physically okay. She blames herself for not being able to keep Rossi from taking Jane."

"It's not her fault. She tried."

"She said the only reason he didn't take her too is that he didn't realize she couldn't walk. She would've slowed him down."

"I'm grateful he didn't take her or Mercy. The situation could be a hell of a lot worse than it is."

"We're going to get both of them back," he says.

"I hope you're right. I know one thing, if we don't, I'll leave no stone unturned hunting him down even if it takes the rest of my life."

"It's not going to come to that. We'll have them

both safely home tomorrow. You really should try to get some sleep. It's going to be a long night."

I hunker down and close my eyes, but all I see is Jane's face. As strong a woman as she is, she has to be terrified. She has no idea what happened with Mercy, whether she was found or not. I'm thankful for her quick thinking placing the phone in her bag. As outraged as I am he took my wife, I would've lost my mind had he taken Mercy too. He warned me he would one day. I let my guard down when my gut told me not to. Tally was the unknown factor. I hope she rots in jail.

CHAPTER TWENTY FIVE

JANE

"Make sure you park in the woods where I told you, then bring her in here," Rossi tells someone on his phone. "You awake? We have company."

I sit and carefully move my leg off the couch. "Someone else you want to torture," I mutter.

"You could say that."

My heart skips a beat. I was being flippant.

He opens the cabin door and stands on the wooden porch, sipping on a cup of coffee. "Did she give you any trouble?"

"Nah, but I had to gag her. She won't shut up." I hear a man's voice.

Picking up the crutches, I hobble to the window.

What I see drops hot coals in the pit of my belly. "Winnie."

Rossi hands him an envelope full of cash and tells the man to leave and never come back. Then he shoves Winnie in the door. Tears fill her eyes when she sees me. She rushes over, and I hug her for a brief second, then pull the gag from her mouth.

"How?" I simply ask.

"I was at the shop, and that tyrant came in the back door and knocked me over before I even knew what happened."

I work at untying her hands.

"Oh no you don't." Rossi steps between us. "She's staying tied up."

"Why? Where's she going to go? It will be dark out soon." I press him.

"I'll untie her so she can eat."

"You expect us to eat!" Winnie snaps.

He pulls his weapon from the back of his pants. "You'll do whatever I damn well tell you to do."

I place my body between him and Winnie. "Leave her alone."

"Come sit." He waves the gun at the small square table in the kitchen.

"Do as he says," I tell Winnie.

When she sits, he removes the rope from around her wrist. She winces as she rubs the reddened area.

"I need to clean her wounds," I snarl.

"She'll be fine," he says, opening the freezer. "I'm not much of a cook. Microwave pot pies will have to do."

"I've done whatever you've asked. Why is she here?" Anger drips from my tone.

"I told you I'd take everything from Ethan. His mother is part of the process," he retorts.

"Let Jane go. I'll take her place," Winnie cries.

"How sweet, trying to bargain with me. You're lucky I don't like kids or that daughter of yours would be here too." He puts the food in the microwave and logs in the time, pressing start.

"Are you alright?" I ask Winnie, reaching over to hold her hand.

"A few bumps and bruises. You look terrible, sweetie."

"I think my knee is broken."

"Did he do that to your face?"

I nod.

"My son will not let you get away with this!" she croaks with outrage.

"Ethan has no idea what's headed his way. The rest of my plan will wait until morning."

"What are you going to do to him?" I pound my fist on the table.

"His job will be gone. Tally has already promised it to one of my men. The house you live in will be burnt to the ground. His best friend, Clem, will not live to see another day."

"You bastard!" I dive at him and stumble to the ground. Winnie helps me to my feet.

"You're really beginning to annoy me. If you don't behave, I'll lock you in the shed out back." The microwave beeps. "Sit down and eat before I force-feed you." He hands us the food with plastic forks. He sits, watching.

"Aren't you joining us?" Winnie asks.

"I'm not eating this crap." He stands, turns to a cabinet and pulls out a bottle of whiskey. "Do you want a drink?" he asks over his shoulder.

"It's all yours," I say.

He pours a large glass and downs it in one gulp, then pours another, sitting back at the table. "My condolences, ma'am. I understand you just lost your husband." He raises his glass in the air.

Winnie, as quick as a cat, lifts her hand and slaps the glass from his hand, sending the whiskey splashing in his face. He places the glass down, gets up, grabs a dishtowel, and wipes his face. "You are spending the night in the shed," he says with a menacing calmness.

"No," I gasp. "You can't put her out there by herself."

"You're more than welcome to go with her." He glares arrows at me.

"I'm not letting her go by herself," I shoot back.

"I've changed my mind. You'll be in my bed tonight."

"Don't you lay a hand on her!" Winnie's voice has a sharp bite.

"That's it, old lady. I've had about enough of you." He gets his gun back out. "Get up."

I know she's afraid when I see her hands shake. "Walk," he orders. He takes her out the side door. I hobble as fast as I can behind him. He unlocks the shed and pushes her inside, locking it again before I make it to her.

"Please don't do this," I beg. "I promise she won't be any trouble."

Winnie is beating on the wall. "Let me out!"

My crutches fall against the shed when he picks me up over his shoulder, carrying me back to the house. He moves into his bedroom, throwing me on the bed. "You are going to sit there and shut your mouth! Not another word!" His jaw flexes back and forth with his hands alternate making a fist. He leaves the room then comes back with the whiskey, guzzling it from the bottle.

If he passes out, I can make my escape.

He takes his phone out of his pocket and places it on the charger next to his keys in a tray on his dresser.

"Is this your cabin?"

"It was my old man's."

"Were the two of you close?"

"You could say that. He taught me everything I know."

"Nice guy, then."

He spins on his heel. "Better than your old man. He deserted you."

"Think what you will. He was a good man. He loved his family to a fault."

He walks into the bathroom to brush his teeth.

I look around for anything I can use as a weapon. Silently, I open his bedside drawer. Nothing but a couple of old books.

He moves toward me, holding another rope. "Hold your hands out."

He ties them and then fastens the other end to the bedpost. "You're lucky I'm too damn tired to touch you."

CHAPTER TWENTY FIVE

My lungs fill with a sigh of relief.

"Lay down."

"I need a light on to sleep." If there is any chance Ethan is out there, he won't be able to see this place in the pitch dark.

"Lady, I am the boogie man," he says, reaching for the lamp.

"Please, it's not like I can go anywhere."

"I'll give you this one." He yanks his shirt off but leaves his jeans on with his gun tucked in the front of them. "Get some sleep. We have a big day tomorrow."

As I hear him snore, I work at my bindings. The rope tears into my skin with every twist and turn. I tug hard, and it loosens. I stop when he sucks in a breath of air and rolls to his stomach. His snore starts again, and I slink out of bed. Standing over him, there's no way I can get the gun without waking him.

Pain shoot through my leg as I use the wall to help me walk over to the dresser. I grab his phone and keys, tucking them into my pocket. The rest of the house is dark. Slowly I make my way to the side door and open it without making a noise. My movements are slow as a turtle makes my way to the shed. It's so dark I'm going on memory. Taking out the keys, I unlock the shed and pick up my crutches still lying on the ground.

"Winnie, it's me," I say quietly. "Where are you?"

A flashlight shines in my face. "Over here."

"We have to get out of here." I take his phone out of my pocket, but it's locked by facial recognition. "Dang it." I toss it in a rusted-out bucket.

"I found a way out, but I wasn't leaving without you."

She stands. "There's a panel that opens under this box." She shines the light.

"How do you know it goes anywhere? Did you open it?"

"Why else would it be in here?"

I brace myself on the crutch and help her push it out of the way. Lifting the handle, the door opens. She shines a light down into it.

"It's a secret passage," she says.

"This is how he moves in and out of here without being seen. I bet his father used it."

"Can you manage the stairs?" She shines the light on my leg.

"I don't have any other choice."

"I'll go first and help you." She hands me the flashlight and lowers herself in the opening. I keep the light shining on her. "Toss me the light," she holds out her hands and catches it. "Go slow."

I get on the ground, put all my weight on my arms and inch myself downward, dragging my crutches with me.

"Where do you think this leads?" The light swings toward the dark passageway.

"I don't know, but we're about to find out." I run my hand on the rough walls for stability. It feels like it's made of wood and mud. Roots from the trees protrude from the walls and floor, making it harder to walk.

"What's that noise?" Winnie asks, shining the light toward it.

"Rats," I say. "Big ones." Winnie takes my elbow. My shoulders scrap the narrow passageway as we make our way through the small space.

"Yuck! A spiderweb." She runs her hand down her face trying to remove the web.

I can hear my panicked breath in my ears playing a fierce melody. Stopping, I take a few deep breaths to calm myself. "We have to keep moving. He'll know where we are when he sees the shed open."

"Why do you think he locked me in there if he knew this passageway was here?"

"He probably thought you wouldn't look and cower in the corner all night."

"He underestimates us Calhoun women," her tone is filled with pride.

"That was his first mistake," I say. "We can't wait for Ethan to rescue us. It's up to us to stay alive."

"I just hope the batteries in this old flashlight don't give out." She shakes it when it starts to blink.

"More reason for us to keep moving."

The air is moldy and hot. I'm not sure how far we've gone because of me ambling slowly. "Winnie. Why don't you walk ahead. You can get out and get help."

"I'm not leaving you. We do this together, or we don't do it at all."

"Did Daddy know what a remarkable woman you are?"

"He did, and I was lucky to have him as long as the Lord allowed it."

We continue to walk. "I feel a breeze blowing in our direction," I point out.

"You're right. I feel it too." We move a little faster. "I see stairs," she shines her light.

I hold on to a wood beam protruding from the wall while she climbs up. "It's too heavy. I can't open it."

I put my full weight on the beam, and it snaps. "I'll help you push." I manage to climb up behind her. Placing the broken end of the beam on the door, we both push. It creaks open, and she's able to get it all the way open.

She climbs out, and I follow her. "It's just as dark out here."

She swings the light around. "I don't see the cabin."

"Good. Let's see if we can find shelter out of sight."

"There's nothing out here but trees," she shines the flashlight out in front of us.

"There's a lot of woods out here. We'll find some-place to hide until the sun starts to peek out."

We walk in step with one another, deeper into the camouflage of the trees.

"I don't even want to think about the critters out here. I sure wish I had Chet's shotgun right about now."

"Me too."

CHAPTER TWENTY SIX

DODGE

*W*hen I make it to the vineyard, the sun is sitting lower in the sky. Rose has her head under the hood of her car, and she's swearing like a sailor. She peeks around the hood when she hears me pull up beside her.

"Thank goodness. My battery is dead. I've been on the phone with Mama, and she's frantic for me to get to the ranch," she rambles all in one breath.

"I guess this is the reason you weren't at the Magnolia like your dad told me. Don't worry about your car. I'll take you. Do you need to grab anything?"

She opens the door to her car, reaches over the backseat and pulls out a small bag. "This is all I need." Slamming the hood of her car, she runs to the passenger side of my car and jumps in.

"Have you heard anything else? I can't believe this is happening. This family has been through enough with losing Grandpa."

"All I know is Boone, Wyatt, and Ethan are headed to Tennessee to find Jane. Rossi's father owned a cabin in the woods up there."

"You think that's where he took her?" She angles her body toward me.

"That's the only lead they have."

"I want to go to my mother's, not the Magnolia," she blurts out before I take a left on the road headed to the bed-and-breakfast.

"Alright, but call your father and let him know."

"Have you called your brother to give him a heads-up?"

"Yes. They have several of the ranch hands guarding the property with rifles."

"Good," she says, calling her father.

I keep an eye out the rearview mirror to make sure there is no one falling me just as a precaution. Rose looks even more panicked when she hangs up with Boone. "Grandma Winnie is missing." She can't stop the flow of tears from streaming.

"Your dad thinks Rossi took her?"

"It appears that way." She lays her head in my lap and curls her legs on the seat.

"I guess if he wants Ethan to pay, kidnapping his wife and mother is one way to do it."

She pops up. "Where's Mercy?" Horror fills her eyes.

"She's safe."

"Thank God." She holds her hand over her chest.

"I'm going to keep you safe, too, Rose." My gaze flitters to her.

"I'm not worried about me. Besides, my daddy taught me how to shoot as well as any man." She takes a pistol from her bag.

"Jane and Winnie both know how to handle a gun. That didn't stop Rossi from disarming them."

"Momma said she was taking River back to their house. Bear was going to keep an eye out for them."

"She should've stayed at the main house. There's safety in numbers."

"She didn't want River to be frightened. She thought he'd do better in his own bed."

An idea crosses my mind thinking about Rossi's goal of revenge on Ethan. "Aren't your mother and Ethan best friends?"

Her brows furrow together. "Yea, why?" Before I answer her, I can see her brain click in. "Drive faster!" She bangs on the dashboard. She whips out her phone and calls her again. "Mom, please stay put at the main house," she says in a rush. By her response, Clem is already home. "Lock the doors. We're on our way."

While she hangs on the phone with Clem, I call Bear. "Hey, man. If Rossi is out to make Ethan pay, you need to go to Clem's house. They're best friends, and she may be on the list of targets for him."

"I'll head there now."

"We'll be there in a few minutes." I disconnect the line.

It's dark by the time I pull onto Whiskey River Road. "I'm dropping you off at the main house."

"Like hell you are! I'm going with you."

I stop at the main entrance. "It's safer for you here."

"If you don't take me with you, I'll walk." Her hand is on the handle to open the door.

"Fine, but you need to stay in the car with the doors locked until I check things out." I push it in drive and take the path leading to Clem's house around the back of the property.

My phone rings. I pick it up and hear Bear. "Turn off your headlights." It sounds as if he's whispering. "There are two men prowling around on the back of the property. Get Rose safely inside, then meet me at the gate on the east end of the house."

"Will do," I say, killing the lights and turning off the engine.

"What did he say?" She's unbuckling her seat belt.

"There are two men on the property that don't belong. He wants you inside the house, and I'm going to help him."

She takes the clip from her gun and counts the rounds, then slaps it back in place. "I'm going with you."

"Would you just for once do as you're told."

"There's one thing you haven't learned about me yet. I'm my own woman, and I'll fight fiercely to save my family and this land. It's something my Grandfather instilled in me, and I'm not running tail when things get tough."

She opens the door. "Your father is going to kill me if anything happens to you."

"Then buckle up, buttercup. You better make sure I don't die." We both close the doors quietly. I take the lead to the gate, where Bear is hunkered down out of sight from the back of the property.

"I told you to take Rose inside," he snarls.

"I'm not one to do as I'm told. Besides, this is my mother and brother inside."

"You are as stubborn as your mother," he huffs softly.

"What's the plan?" I ask.

"They've been sitting near the fence line puffing on cigarettes, so they haven't made their move yet. I want you and Calamity Jane here to go to the opposite side of me. Rose, you make your way to the back porch. Dodge, you hang to the side. My guess is they'll divide and conquer. One will head to the front and one through the back. You stop the one in the back. Rose, you're set up in case Dodge can't stop him. I'll take the other one out in the front."

"See, you did need me," Rose says.

"It looks like one of them is gone." I point.

"Get in place. I'll find him," Bear orders.

Rose and I slink around the front to move down the fence line on the other side. Rose bends between the railings and takes off in a run to the back porch. I squat low to keep trained on the other man.

"You've seriously miscalculated," a deep low voice says from behind me.

I look over my shoulder and see a guy dressed in all black with a ski mask on holding a high-powered weapon. A man runs behind him, moving toward the front of the house.

"There's three of you," I say. Which means Rose is

in danger. Rising to my feet ever so slowly with my hands in the air, he tells me to lay my rifle down. Grasping in my left hand, I toss it, and when I do, I keep the momentum with my body and swing around with my right hand balled in a fist, punching him in the face while kicking his feet out from beneath him. Pummeling on top of him, I gain control of his weapon. With the butt of it, I smash it into his head, knocking him out. I pick up my rifle and whirl around to gain sight of the man that was on the back of the property. He's not there. Jumping the fence, I take off in a sprint to the porch. I hear a gunshot which has me running harder. When I make it to the porch, the man is lying a few feet out in the grass, and Rose is still aiming her gun.

She hears me running in the dirt and wheels her gun toward me. "It's me," I say, and she drops her gun. She barrels down the steps into my arms. "Thank God, you're okay." I kiss her forehead.

"I've never killed a man before," she cries.

As I hug her, I glance in his direction, and he's still moving. "He's not dead," I say, releasing her, walking toward him. She landed a hit to his right side, and he's wallowing in pain, rolling in the grass. As I stand over him, I keep my gun on him. Another gunshot blares into the darkness.

"Uncle Bear!" Rose yells, taking off in a run.

"Rose!" I holler after her, but she doesn't stop.

I grasp the man by his shirt, hauling him to his feet as he yells out in pain. I drag him to the front of the house, where I see Bear hovering over a dead body. I drop him beside him.

"There is a third man." As I say the words, the third guy comes out of the dark, gripping a sidearm. Blood trickles in his left eye. He looks down for a split second at his men, and I lift my weapon and pull the trigger. His body bounces with the multiple hits before he falls to the ground with a thud.

Clem, who had been watching out of the window, comes running out and straight into Rose's arms. "He could have killed you," she bellows.

"I'm alright, mom. We're all safe." Rose tries to calm her. "Thanks to Uncle Bear and Dodge."

"Thanks to you, too," I add. "If your stubborn ass wouldn't have insisted on helping, one of them would've gotten inside," I squeeze her arm.

"Let's get you and River back to the main house," Bear insists. I've got our men surrounding it. You're a sitting duck back here by yourself."

Clem finally relents and gathers River in her arms.

Bears phone vibrates, and he pulls it out of his pocket. He listens, then hangs up. "Shit."

"What now?" Clem asks.

"Ian said they caught a few men trying to set fire to Wyatt's house."

Roses gasps. "Did they stop them?"

"Yes, but I need to send a few of our men to help."

"I'll go," I volunteer.

"If you're going, so am I," Rose barks.

Clem steps up to her. "I need you to stay and help with the kids. Please don't put yourself in any more harm's way."

"I agree. Let the men handle it." Bear props his hand on her shoulder. "I'm sure with that aim of yours, you could help at the main house."

"Fine, but I ain't sitting in some corner being scared. I'll post outside with the ranch hands." She marches to my car.

"That girl is more and more like Boone every single day." Bear shakes his head.

"He'd be proud, but she scares the heck out of me," Clem says, headed to her truck.

I walk around it and look in the back, making sure someone didn't sneak inside. "You're good," I say, slapping my hand on the back panel of the truck.

"Follow them to make sure they're safe." He

hands me a walkie talkie. "Channel five will get you Ian. Tell him I'll send two additional men. It's all I can spare. I'll contact Mike and keep an eye on this one until he gets here." He nudges the injured guy with his boot, and he groans.

I nod, getting in my car.

"Dodge," Bear says.

"Thanks for help keeping our family safe."

"You bet. I'd say anytime, but I'm hoping like heck this is the last time this family has any issues. Probably not, but a man can hope.

CHAPTER TWENTY SEVEN

ETHAN

*T*he night has been long. The sun should be up in the next hour. I've seen no movement from the house. The one single light is still on. Wyatt and Boone have taken turns napping. Boone is stressed because there's no cell service on this tower, and he hasn't been able to check on his family.

"I'm going to walk out a ways and see if I can't get service," he says, climbing down the stairs of the tower.

Wyatt stirs, sitting up. "Where's he going?" he yawns.

"To find a spot he can make a call."

"Good idea," he stands, following him.

My focus goes back on the cabin, and I see a man

inside walk by the window. I take out my binoculars to get a better look. He walks by the window several times, but I can't make out his face because his back is to me. "Come on, turn around," I say. He disappears, and I don't see him until he's standing in the front door, holding a gun.

"It's Rossi," I choke, scrambling to my feet.

Wyatt fumbles up the stairs. "It's him?" He grabs the binoculars from my hand, aiming them toward the cabin. "I'll be damned. Dodge and Molly were right."

I stuff our belongings in the bag and guzzle down a bottle of water. "We've got to get to him."

"Wait," Wyatt says. "He's looking for something." He hands them back to me.

I watch him walk behind the house. He's mouthing something as he storms toward the shed. He glares at the padlock on the ground, then nearly rips off the door opening it with his gun in the air. He runs inside and, a few minutes later, runs back out headed for the house.

"Jane and Winnie must've been inside that shed, and they escaped." I bolt down the stairs with Wyatt steps behind me. I nearly bowl over Boone when I hit the ground. He doesn't ask questions. We climb in the truck, and I pull up the navigation to take us to Rossi's cabin.

"There's no easy access, according to this. I know there's a way there because of the delivery truck parked outside."

"Get as close as you can, and we'll go the rest of the way on foot," Boone states.

"Jane and Winnie seemed to escape. One of us should check the surrounding area."

"I'll do it," Wyatt responds. "You two go after Rossi."

I follow the GPS map that leads me further into the woods, but the path ends. Parking, we all get out and suit up, armed with our vests and weapons. "Each of us has a walkie-talkie. If you find anything, go to channel five like we use as the ranch."

"I suggest we stay together until we can get a lead on which direction the girls headed," Boone says.

"We'll swarm the house and go from there," I respond. "If you find Rossi before we find the women, don't kill him."

"That's a given." Wyatt locks and loads his gun.

"You two that way." Boone points. "Wyatt, over there. I'll take the back."

Each of us split in the direction Boone ordered.

When I come to a break in the trees, I see the

cabin. The front door is wide open, and the truck is still parked out front. As stealthily as I can, I place my boot on the front step without a noise. Shuffling inside with my weapon held high, I sweep the house. There is bloody gauze lying on the coffee table. Edging my way into the bedroom, I see ropes tinged with blood torn from the bed. A half-empty whiskey bottle is on the far bedside table.

My radio cracks. Tugging it from my hip. I press the button to listen. "I have something in the shed," Boone growls.

"I'll be right there. The house is empty."

Boone and Wyatt are standing outside the shed when I got out the side door. "There's a tunnel. This must be how they escaped." Boone opens the door wider.

I shine my light in the hole. "Damn." I look up when I hear the sound of a dirt bike starting up. The three of us run toward the sound to see Rossi popping a wheelie, taking off into the woods. "I'll follow him!" I yell, already in motion. "You find out where that tunnel leads!" I tuck my firearm into the holster.

My feet hit the dirt hard as I weave my way around trees trying not to lose sight of Rossi. The forest slows him down, but he still has a better pace on me. As I stop to catch my breath, I see a path that angles down and around. He's following it on the bike. There's a straight path down to where he's going. It's steep, and it's going to hurt like hell if I fall. I don't see any other way of catching him. Bending my knees, I dig my boots in the ground and try to keep my balance and not trip over a root as I shift my momentum downward. I slip and land hard against a tree. I don't waste time getting to my feet. I see Rossi rounding the corner. If I move fast enough, I can catch him at the bottom.

I don't think; I just run. At the last steep end, Rossi has come to a straighter path and has shifted into high gear. I time it right, and right before he's underneath me, I jump, hitting him hard. The bike goes one way, and we go another. He grunts as his body smacks against a large tree. I roll a few feet away.

I reach for my gun and find it not in its holster. Glancing around, I don't see it.

Rossi slowly gets up, holding his side. "How the hell did you find me?" he snaps.

"Where are my wife and mother?" I'm on my feet, aiming to knock him off his.

He whips out a gun, and I stop cold in my tracks. "This isn't how I wanted this to go down." He aims the gun, and I feel the bullet hit my chest, knocking me completely off my feet and falling down the side of the mountain. The last thing I remember is my head smashing against a rock.

I wake to the sound of my radio. "I found him," Boone says. His large hands roll me over. Dirt and blood sting my eye. "Did you get shot?" He's feeling my chest. He rips open my shirt to bear the vest. "You're lucky you were wearing this." He grasps either side of the vest with his hands, hauling me to my feet. "Wyatt went down the tunnel and found footprints. There's two sets. We have to get them before Rossi does."

My head spins, and I feel dizzy. I stumble, and Boone catches me. "You need to suck it up or sit it out," he barks.

"I'm fine." I jerk myself away from him.

"Then get your ass in gear." He takes off running, and I follow him.

Wyatt though the walkie-talkie, leads us to him. "Looks like they took off that way." He points.

"I'll hang to the side to keep an eye out for Rossi. You two follow the tracks. It appears one of them is walking on crutches by the pattern in the dirt. They couldn't have moved very fast or gone far. Check under down trees for anywhere they may have hidden."

I want to yell her name, but if Rossi is anywhere near them and she calls back, he'll take her down. "He doesn't want me dead. He wants me to suffer. Killing either one of them in front of me, he would accomplish his goal. I lost gun when I fell," I tell Wyatt.

He pulls one out of his boot, handing it to me. "Try not to lose this one." He grins.

Moving several feet apart, we keep our weapons trained out in front of us. We slowly make our way further into the thick woods. We take our time searching one area before we move to the next. I see a small piece of fabric hanging on the bark of a tree. I motion for Wyatt to follow me. We are about a half mile in when I hear a noise. Pressing a finger to my lips, I let Wyatt know not to make a sound. Raising my elbow, I rest my hand holding my gun on it to get a better aim. I inch my way over to a downed tree, and I peer over it. I see a wisp of blond hair.

"Jane," I call out.

Her head pops up, and she drops the large rock she had grasped in her hand. "Ethan! I knew you'd find us."

Winnie stands with tears in her eyes. "Her leg is injured," she says, choking back tears.

As I go to climb down, a shot rings out, barely missing me, stopping my movement. "Get down!" I yell.

"I don't have eyes on him," Wyatt says, finding a place on the ground.

I rip the walkie from my pants. "Boone, please tell me you see him."

"Not yet."

Staying close to the ground, I work my way down to Jane. Anger boils in my gut like a live volcano. Her face is bruised, and she can barely open her eye. Her leg is in a splint but painfully swollen. Both her wrists and my mother's look as if they've been through a meat grinder. Jane clings to my neck.

"I would never leave you," is the first thing she says.

"I know, darling." I push the button on the walkie-talkie again. "I want to be the one that kills him," I warn. A shot goes off again near my mother. She falls to the ground out of fear.

"I have him in my crosshairs," Boone says over the walkie-talkies. "Do you want me to kill him or not?"

"No. Shoot him where it will only cause pain," I snarl.

I stare at Jane. "Do you want me to kill him or send him to prison?"

"Kill him," she doesn't hesitate with her answer. "If you don't, he'll escape again."

I nod. "Stay low," I respond to Boone. "Now." Instantaneously his rifle blares.

A scream followed by a hard hit to the ground is next. Rossi is a few hundred yards out. Hustling over to him before he has a chance to get up, I stand looking down at him with my gun. Boone landed a square shot in his shoulder.

Rossi cuts his eyes in the direction of his rifle. "You can reach for it to try to save your sorry ass, but either way, it doesn't end well for you."

"You've been nothing but a pain in my ass for years! I should've killed her the minute I laid my hands on her along with that brat of yours!"

I rock my head side to side, clenching my jaw. Shifting my boot toward his rifle, I slide it toward him. He stares at me for a hard minute. The look I give him says his time is up. He can either have one last chance to take me out or die.

He snatches his rifle, and I wait until the last possible second when he's looking me in the eye, and I pull the trigger. A single shot to the forehead has him slumping over.

"One moment longer, and I was going to pull the trigger myself," Boone says, walking up behind me. "I'll take care of him. You go to the girls."

I run over to Jane, helping her off the ground, hugging her. "It's over. It's finally over. You'll never have to look over your shoulder again." I grab my mother holding her too.

"Thank you," my mother sobs.

"Where is Mercy?" Jane wails. "Did you find her?"

"She's safe. Thanks to your quick thinking of putting your phone in her bag, I tracked her to Tally's place."

"She took her to her house?" Her voice rises. "How stupid is she?" She tried to convince me she saved our daughter from Rossi when he kidnapped you."

"I hope she burns in hell," my mother says.

"What she said." Jane giggles.

Wyatt helps my mom maneuver back up the mountain, and I carry Jane in my arms. "I'm so sorry. He made me tell you I was leaving you."

"I know, darling. I trust you. I knew something had to be wrong."

Her eyes grow large. "He said he was going to kill Clem and burn down our house."

I set her on a rock and snag the walkie. "Boone, did you get ahold of Clem earlier?"

"Yes. Everyone is okay. Bear, Dodge, and Rose saved Clem from Rossi's men. Ian and a brood of men wrangled men on Wyatt's property that were instructed by Rossi to burn it down."

"Thank God." Jane sighs.

"Sorry, I didn't get to tell you earlier," he says.

"Are you carrying his body back to the house?"

"No. I'm disposing it so he'll never be found."

I rest the radio on my forehead. "I should be taking care of it."

"You take care of Jane and your mother. I got this. The bastard tried to kill my wife."

"We'll see you back at the truck."

Picking up Jane again. I make the trek upward. "I'm curious. How did you find the tunnel?"

"Your mother did. Rossi locked her in the shed, thinking she'd cower. Instead, she used her head to try and find a way out. She's one awesome lady. If it weren't for her, he'd still have us bound, and lord knows what he would've done to us and you." She braces her hand on my cheek.

CHAPTER TWENTY EIGHT

ROSE

"*D*on't open your eyes until I tell you to," Dodge helps me out of my car. I lift my head up, trying to see out of the bottom of the blindfold. "I said no peeking." He laughs.

"I hate surprises," I grumble.

"You're going to like this one." My hand settles into his, giving in. Once he has me where he wants, I feel him standing in front of me. "You can take it off now."

I lick my lips in anticipation and raise my hands, removing the bandanna from my eyes. He steps out of the way so I can see.

"Whose place is this?" I ask, looking around while I take the three steps up to the porch.

When I whirl around, Dodge is down on one

knee. My hand covers my gaping mouth. "What are you doing?"

He's holding a small black velvet box in the palm of his hand. "This place is ours, if you'll say yes."

I prop one leg out and cross my arms over my blouse. "Whose place is it if I say no?"

"It will be mine until you finally give in to me and say yes. You're killing me." He stands. "It's not far from the vineyard. Actually, if you go to the back of the property, you can see it."

"I...well..." I wring my hands together, trying to find the words. "I don't want to answer you until I know if I have cancer or not."

"Whether you have the C-word or not doesn't change the fact that I want you to be my wife." He hands me an envelope. "I hope you like being married to a poor man."

I scowl. "What are you talking about?"

"Open the letter."

Ripping it open, my gaze grazes the letter. "You didn't?"

"I did. I paid cash for this place and then donated all my money to the breast cancer research foundation."

"You did this before we even found out?" My mouth falls open for the second time.

"Rose, either way, it's a good cause. Think of how many women this could help."

I throw my arms around his neck. "I love you. Thank you."

"So you don't mind me being broke." He chuckles.

"You're a smart man. You'll find something to turn to gold. Besides, we have what I make off the vineyard."

He pulls back to look at me. "I will not be a kept man, but does this mean your answer is yes?" He holds out the box again.

I flip the lid open. "I don't want to fight my feelings for you anymore. You've proven to me and my family that you're a good man regardless of the things you've done in the past. Part of me always thought we'd end up together. I think we both had a lot of growing up to do before that could happen. The last few weeks since the ordeal with Jane and Ethan have grounded me in the family even more. As long as you promise we never have to leave here, then you can put that ring on my finger."

He takes it out of the box. "I promise not to be the man I used to be. I only want to be the man you need and love. You can count on me to always keep you safe and love you. I'm not promising perfection by any means, but I will work every day of the rest of my life to make you happy and proud to call me your husband."

"I'm already proud of you. But, are you a hundred percent sure you want to be part of my family? We're a pretty tough crowd. We have lots of secrets, most of them not good. You've seen what we're capable of."

"I was there. I know exactly what I'm getting into. A family that fiercely loves one another. I didn't have that growing up. I need you and your entire brood." He slips the silver band with a delicate, beautiful diamond onto my finger. I couldn't have picked a better one out for myself. "It's Perfect." I quirk a brow at him. "Did you ask my daddy for my hand in marriage?"

"I did. And, I went and had a chat with your grandfather too. I know he'd approve. Oh, and speaking of your father, he's on his way out here. He didn't sound none too happy when he called me for your whereabouts."

"Crap. I've been trying to avoid him."

"Why?" His brow furrows.

"Because with everything that happened, I canceled my appointment, and I just haven't had time to reschedule it."

"Then please let me hear the word yes you'll marry me before he gets here and tans your hide."

I snort. "Yes, I'll marry you. I'm a little too old for tan hiding from my daddy, but you, on the other hand, I'd be willing to try." As I kiss him, I hear the roar of my daddy's diesel truck barreling up the driveway. "You shouldn't have told him where we were."

"I'm not getting in the way of your father." He laughs.

"Rose!" Daddy shouts.

"Calm down, Daddy." I press my hands on his chest when he's in front of me.

"You canceled your test. I called Doc, and he rearranged his schedule to see you this afternoon."

"I'm capable of making my own appointment."

"Evidently not," he growls.

"You're ruining a romantic moment between me and Dodge. He bought this house and land for us."

"That's nice. Get your ass in my truck."

"Daddy," I say, then stare at Dodge. "Aren't you going to do something about this?"

"I guess I can carry you to his truck, so he doesn't drag you." He lifts a shoulder.

"Fine!" I huff. "But, if you want to be my husband, you're going to have to grow a pair of bigger balls," I yell over my shoulder before slamming the door to the truck.

Daddy gets in, snickering. "Damn, you get your mouth from your mother." He starts the engine. "You don't really expect Dodge to stand against me when I have your best interest at heart, do you?"

"No," I mutter.

"Good."

"Did he really ask you for my hand in marriage?"

"He did. He was a little nervous, and of course, I gave him a hard time, but he didn't back down. He'll be good for you. You do love him?" He stares at me.

"Yes, yes I do."

"I don't think there's another man alive that could handle you or your family."

I watch the bluegrass of Kentucky roll by my window.

"Are you scared?"

"About getting married or the test?"

"Both."

"I've got fine examples all around me of what it takes to be married. I'm not afraid of that. The results of the test are another story. I don't want to burden Dodge, and I don't want to be disfigured."

"That boy will love you no matter what."

"I know he will, but it still frightens me."

He parks the truck alongside Doc's office. He reaches over, holding my hand before we get out. "We're all here for you."

"Thanks, Daddy."

***

OVER THE NEXT couple of hours, Doc has sent me to the hospital to have a biopsy, blood work, and to pee in a cup. He said he wanted to make sure to check me from head to toe, seeing how difficult it was to get me in his office.

I'm sitting on the metal table in one of his rooms, waiting for him to give me all the results. Daddy has been sitting in the corner of the room, flipping through a fishing magazine.

Doc walks in holding my chart. "Would you like me to go over the results privately?" he asks.

My stomach rolls with nausea, and I break out into a sweat. Daddy stands beside me. "No. I want him here with me." He holds my hand.

"Your shoulder has healed nicely. The tests showed no tumor. It was caused by your fall."

"I blow out a breath of relief. "Thank goodness."

Doc's lips are pinched together. "There is one test that came back positive."

That brief relaxation is smothered by fear. "What is it?"

"You're pregnant. From my best guess is about eight weeks."

I snatch the paper from his hands. "It can't be. The test is wrong. I'm on the pill."

"I confirmed it with your blood work." He points to a line in the chart.

"No…no…no. I can't be pregnant."

Doc looks at Daddy. "Who knew this would be bad news?"

"It's okay, Doc. Give me a minute with her."

I pace the small room. "I don't want kids, do I?" I'm asking myself. "A kid was never in the plan." I hold my belly and see the ring Dodge put on my finger. "Dodge," I say in a long breath.

"It is Dodge's, right?" Daddy asks, holding on to my shoulders.

"Of course, it's Dodge's. It had to be…"

Daddy quirks a brow at me. "The first day he came back to town. That would explain the red mark on your neck that morning."

"What am I going to do? We both specifically said no children. Just the two of us."

"Why would Dodge have bought a big house if he didn't want to fill it with children?"

"He wanted to tear it down and build a small one. He gave away all his money," I huff.

"Please, sit down. Let's talk about this."

The door opens, and Doc rolls in an ultrasound machine. "I thought maybe you'd want to see the little one growing in your belly."

"I don't know, do I?" I ask my father.

He pats the paper-covered table. "Let's just make sure everything is okay."

I sit on the edge, then lie back, pulling up my blouse to show my belly. Doc puts gel on the probe and rolls it low on my stomach. I hear a swishing noise. "What's that?"

"It's the baby's heartbeat," Daddy says, running his hand on the top of my head.

A feeling I've never felt rushes over me. It's an instant love for a little blip on the screen.

"We can talk about your choices, Rose. I'd like for you to let this all sink in first," Doc states.

I lean over, grab a tissue and wipe the gel from my abdomen. "There's nothing to talk about." I bound off the hard bed. Storming out, I don't stop until I've locked myself into Daddy's truck. A few minutes later, he comes out holding a bag. He gets in and doesn't say a word for the first few minutes.

"Do you want to talk about it?"

I cup my belly. "I'm having a baby. I may lose Dodge over it, but hearing the baby's heartbeat, I could never get rid of it. This wave of love filled me."

"Do you want me to talk to Dodge?"

"No. You'd only try to persuade him. He's made it clear he doesn't want kids."

"I've seen Dodge change in a matter of weeks. He did it because he loves you."

"Yea, but a baby is a whole other ball game. You can't make a man want a child."

"Up until twenty minutes ago, you never wanted one. I'm just saying, you need to give him a chance."

I lean my head on the window.

"Do you want me to take you to your mother? Maybe a female perspective would be better than mine."

Lifting my head, I touch his hand. "You were the perfect one to be with me today. Momma would've been all teary-eyed with happiness and not let me feel whatever I needed to feel. You let me be me, and I love you for it."

"I'm glad I could be there for you."

"There's so much to work out. I'm going to have

to hire more help at the vineyard when the baby comes."

"You'll figure it out. You can run a successful business and have a family. Dodge has been a big help with it. He'll pick up the day-to-day things quickly. He's a smart man."

"I guess it depends if he sticks around or not."

CHAPTER TWENTY NINE

DODGE

"She said yes, man. Can you believe it?" I called my brother to share the good news.

"Honestly, no I can't. Did you get her to sell the vineyard?" There's a hint of a bitter drip in his tone.

"I quit my job weeks ago. I've been helping her grow her business because I want to see her product all over the world. Rose loves what she does, and so do I."

"Wow. I'm impressed."

"I bought us a house on the adjacent property to the vineyard. I'm going to tear down the old house and build us a small home for just the two of us. We could expand the vineyard onto the property if we need to. Maybe even buy a few horses."

"I have to say, I'm happy for you. You're finally

growing roots, and you couldn't have picked a better woman for you. Rose will keep you in line."

"Don't tell Missy, let Rose handle it. She'll want to share the good news herself with her family."

"What are you going to do for work?"

I scratch my head. "I haven't figured it out yet. I'll have to come up with something quick. I donated all my money to a charity in Rose's name."

I hear him spew whatever he was drinking. "You did what?"

"The money was tainted as far as I'm concerned, so it should go to good use."

"So, you're broke, you buy a house, then ask a woman to marry you. Only Dodge Anderson could pull that off." He laughs.

"I want a legit business where I'm not stealing people's dreams."

"I'm sure you'll come up with something."

"First thing I need to do is sell my car and buy a truck."

"Who are you?" He chuckles.

"Go big or go home, right?"

"I'm sure Boone will help you pick one out."

"Give Missy and Morgan my love. Remember, mums the word until Rose spills the beans herself."

"I am happy for you, brother, and I'm glad you'll be living nearby. I'm proud of you."

"Thanks, Tucker." Ian pulls up as I hang up with my brother. I called him to come look at the property. The house needs to come down, and I want some ideas on where to put the new home.

"Hey, Dodge," he says with a handshake.

"Thanks for coming out."

"Molly told me about this place. She said you want to tear it down." We walk the parameter together. "The foundation looks great. Do you mind if I take a look inside?"

"I'll give you a tour. Don't expect much. I bought the place for the land." He follows me inside. Flipping on the overhead light, it flickers a few times before it comes on. The warped fan blades drift loudly clockwise, taking forever to hobble through a final rotation trying to gain momentum. The floorboards bend under the weight of our feet. "The floor is actually sloped downward."

"What a great old fireplace," he says, running his hand along a pine mantel.

"I doubt it's been used in years."

We walk into the kitchen. There's a water stain on the ceiling, grimy window seals, chipped cabinet doors that are hung askew. The sink is rust-stained, an outdated appliance by a century.

Ian squats, peeling up a corner of the water-damaged linoleum. "The floor underneath could use some TLC, but they'd be gorgeous refinished."

"I'm tearing it down, not wanting to renovate."

"Too bad. This place has great bones. The floor could be brought level easily."

Next is the upstairs bathroom. There is exposed plumbing protruding from the shower, and half the tile is either chipped or missing, not to mention the grout lines are blackened with mold.

"This would need a total overhaul." He taps a tile, and it falls into the chipped porcelain tub. "You don't see claw tubs too often anymore. I bet this was a beauty in its day."

"You certainly have an eye of appreciation I don't. I see a costly mess."

We walk the rest of the house with him, pointing out things he thinks are great. "I think you should consider remodeling this house. It will cost money and time, but they don't make them like this anymore. It's got six bedrooms and an office."

"I have no plans on needing six bedrooms. I was thinking a two-bedroom home with an office. Tucker and Missy could stay and bring the baby."

"I'm sure Molly would agree. A three-bedroom home would have better resell value."

"I don't plan on moving."

"You're making this permanent?" he asks.

"Yes. It butts right up to Rose's place."

"Boone told me you asked for Rose's hand in marriage." He claps his hand on my shoulder. "You're a brave man," he snorts.

"He didn't make it easy on me. I would've expected nothing less from a man like Boone."

"Has Rose seen the inside of this place yet?"

"No, her father stole her before she had a chance to come inside."

"Knowing Rose's taste, she'll love this house and want it restored." We walk back outside.

"I was thinking I'd prefer the house built further back on the property amongst the trees. I could fence all this off and build a barn for the horses. That way, the house is a little more secluded. We'd leave the back acreage for growing the vines. That is after I find another job to pay for it."

"I see your point. I'll do whatever you want. I can have this drawn up in no time if you'll email me your ideas on a layout."

"Will do." I shake his hand again.

"Looks like Boone is headed your way," he says, ducking into his truck to leave.

Ian stops to talk to Tucker before he drives off. Boone parks, but they don't get out right away. My stomach turns, thinking Rose is bringing bad news. Whatever it is, we'll handle it together. She finally gets out, and Boone drives off.

"Hey, beautiful," I say, holding my arms out.

She doesn't walk into them. "We need to talk." She sits on the steps of the house, and I join her, draping my arm around her shoulder.

"It's okay, Rose. I'm not going anywhere." I kiss the side of her head.

"It's not what you think." She twists her hands in knots.

"Look at me." She does. "What is it?"

She hops up. "You know, I never got to see the inside of this house because Daddy interrupted us."

I stand. "Alright, then let's go inside." I'm worried she doesn't want to talk.

"Wow, this place is awesome!" Her head moves from side to side, checking out every inch. "She needs a little loving, that's all."

"Ian said you would love it." I chuckle. "I hired him to tear down and build a new place."

"What? No. I love the structure. The high ceilings and the woodwork is fabulous."

"Like I told him, all I see is a mess. A bit of a money pit."

"Please don't take a wrecking ball to this place. She'll take time, but she'll be worth it." She meanders through each room, touching every inch.

"You really want to renovate this place? Where are we going to live until this place is livable."

"We can stay at my place."

"Rose, we don't need a six-bedroom house."

Her mood shifts to sadness. "About that."

I walk over to her, resting my hands on her hips. "Please tell me what the doctor said."

"Do you recall the first day you came to town, and we had sex in the cellar?"

"How could I forget? What does that have to do with you having cancer?"

"The good news is I don't. The lump was caused from the fall."

"I'm not following you, Rose. What does us having sex have to do with anything?"

She digs her hand in her back pocket and hands me a black and white photo. "Doc figures I'm eight weeks pregnant. Daddy had him print the ultrasound picture for me."

I take a large step back. "You're pregnant?"

Her eyes throw daggers at me. "It's our baby."

I run my hand through my hair and blow out a long breath. "I...I need time to think about this."

"What's there to think about, Dodge? I'm pregnant. This isn't the ideal situation, but as soon as I saw our baby and heard the heartbeat, I fell in love."

"You...we..." I point between us. "Don't want kids."

She snatches the picture from my hand. "I thought maybe once you knew, you'd change your mind." She stomps angrily out of the house.

"Just give me some time to think. That's all I'm asking," I holler, following her. "You asked me for time to think about how you felt about me. What's the difference?" I'm holding her car door open so she can't shut it.

"The difference is you said you'd love me no matter what. If you love me, you have to love this baby. Obviously, we're not on the same page." She frees the door from my grasp, slamming it and driving away.

"Damn it!" I kick the dirt with my boot. A baby was definitely not in the plan. I handled the situation all wrong. I was taken completely off guard by her news. Here I was prepared to handle cancer with her. Instead, she tells me she's pregnant. "I have to tell her my reasoning, why I never wanted kids."

Pulling out my phone, I call Ian. "Scratch the building plans. Change them to a remodel," I say and hang up.

CHAPTER THIRTY

JANE

"You've been eerily quiet since the ordeal with Rossi." Ethan is lying in bed with his hand behind his head. The dark circles under his eyes tell me he's not sleeping well. Placing my head on his shoulder, I splay my hand on his bare chest. "Do you want to talk about it?"

He removes my hand, rolling over to look me square in the eye. "Your face has finally healed. There's only a trace of a bruise left." His finger traces my cheekbone, where I'll have a small scar.

"My leg is improving every day. I should be out of this cast in a couple of weeks."

"I'm so sorry, darling." His eyes mist over.

"What are you sorry for, Ethan." I toy with the end of his hair.

"I didn't keep you and Mercy safe like I promised. If I had, none of this would've happened to you."

"You need to quit beating yourself up. You can't be with me twenty-four seven. We both have lives to live. I don't blame you for what happened. That was all on Rossi, and he's never going to hurt any of us again."

"How do you feel about what I did?" His gaze rocks back and forth with mine.

"Not any different than I felt about myself when I took a man's life for hurting this family. You did what you had to do. Things aren't always black and white, Ethan. Sometimes hard choices have to be made, and that's what you did. You did it for me and Mercy."

He takes a deep breath in and blows out as if a weight has been lifted off his chest. "He's out of our lives for good, and Tally will have prison time."

"You know she deserves it, right?"

He turns over on his back. "Yes," he says, staring up at the ceiling. "Part of me feels bad for her."

I sit square in the middle of the bed with one leg straight. "Tell me why?"

"I think she had it in her to be a good person. She was just misguided in her thinking."

"Look. I know you always strive to see the good

in people. What good that was left in Tally was overrun by her own desires. Short of giving in to her, there was nothing you could've done to change the path she chose."

He reaches up, sweeping a lock of hair over my shoulder. "When did you get to be the reasonable one?"

"I learned it from my husband." I laugh, kissing the palm of his hand. "Everything is going to be okay."

"Do you think Mercy will remember any of it?"

"I doubt it, but if she does, I know you'll be there to help her. We both will."

"Thank you for not leaving me." He leans up, placing his sweet lips to mine.

"I promised I'd never run, no matter what. I love you, Ethan. You are my heart."

He lies back down. "I'm glad Wyatt was able to get the money back your father left you."

"Rossi didn't need the money. He only wanted to punish you."

"Have you decided what you're going to do with the money?"

"I'm going to put some of it in a trust for Mercy."

"And the rest of it?"

"I was thinking maybe we could adopt a son." I

bite my bottom lip, not knowing how he's going to feel about it.

He sits cross-legged in front of me. "Are you ready for that? You said before you didn't want to adopt a child."

"I know what I said, but I've changed my mind. I want our family to grow. There is a little boy out there that needs a father like you. We have so much love to give."

The glisten in his eyes turns to tears. "I love you so much." He kisses me hard.

I wipe away his tears. "Is this what you want? I don't want to force you into something you're not comfortable with."

"Yes! Yes!" He lays me on my back, hovering over me. "I do. A million times over, I do. I promise to take care of all of you and keep you safe. I won't let you down."

"You've never let any of us down, Ethan. You saved us. You've saved me a million times over. I can't imagine the woman I'd be without you in my life."

"Cranky like your old man." He nips my nose with his teeth.

"I miss that cranky old man. He'd love knowing he was going to have another grandson."

He rolls off me, sitting on the edge of the bed. "He could be a son of a bitch with adults, but he sure loved the kiddos."

I scooch next to him. "All of us Calhoun women are having lunch with your mom today at the Magnolia."

"Thanks for including her."

"We wouldn't have it any other way. She's part of this family. We all love her. She's endured a lot these last couple of weeks, and she's proven what a strong woman she is. I need her as much as I need anyone in this family."

He stands, tugging on his jeans. "I've got to go to the office. Ian has been appointed acting mayor."

"I think he'll be perfect for the job. No more worrying about whether or not he has to take a job out of town. Ellie is ecstatic."

"For now, he'll continue with both jobs until the position is permanent."

I knock my knuckles on my cast. "I'll sure be glad when this thing is gone so we can get back to our sex life."

"I can work around it." He grins.

"Then why haven't you?" I frown.

"I wasn't sure if you were angry with me or not, and I didn't want to hurt you."

"I was never mad at you, Ethan. I wish we would've talked this out when we got home."

"Me, too." He lifts my chin, kissing me again. "I promise to make it up to you."

"I think you need a spanking for your lack of communication," I tease.

"Not on your life," he snickers. "But, I'd be glad to have my hand on your ass." He adjusts his Stetson on his head.

"You are one fine-looking cowboy." I lick my lips.

"Tell my mother I'll stop by later. You ladies have fun."

Hobbling out of the bedroom, I follow him to Mercy's room. She's lying in her bed playing with her toys. He leans down, giving her a kiss. "Daddy loves you, darling." She squeezes his neck and returns to her toys.

"Have a good day. Tell Ian congrats for me." He pats my ass teasingly as he walks out.

I sit on the end of the bed with Mercy. "You are one lucky little girl to have a daddy that loves you so much." I can't wait to bring home a little brother for her. She loves her cousins so much she'll enjoy having a brother of her own.

I dress Mercy in her favorite pink frilly dress with the cowgirl boots she insists upon wearing every day. She's truly a Calhoun. She plays in my makeup as I pull on a simple flowered dress and one boot. I pack Mercy's bag, hold her hand and stand out on the porch. It feels good to no longer have to look over my shoulder. "We're safe," I say out loud. "Your daddy made sure of it," I tell Mercy.

We load up in the car and drive the Magnolia Mill. Mercy squeals when she sees Margret. She runs and jumps in her lap.

"There's my pretty little niece." She hugs her tight.

Margret and I share a stronger bond than ever before after what we went through. She felt guilty for being left behind and not helping me. We've talked many times about it, and I think she's finally let those feelings go. Mercy runs off to play with her cousins, who've built a fort in the dining room.

Clem, Ellie, Nita, Molly, and Winnie are all around the kitchen counter preparing our lunch. Margret gets out of her wheelchair to stand by all of us. Winnie pours each of us a glass of wine. "I'm so thankful to be part of this family." She lifts her glass, and we all toast.

"Here's to Daddy," Ellie says.

"Yes, to Chet," Nita adds.

"I'm heartbroken he's gone, but I'm thankful he gave us you," Clem says directly to Winnie.

Molly and I lock arms. "We'll all be here for each other. I can give a good lecture like Daddy did, so we don't miss him as much." They all chuckle.

"I half expect all your men to show up like any other of our girls' outings." Winnie looks at each of us.

"We had to make them swear to stay away," Ellie snickers. "We told them we wanted this to be about you."

Winnie sniffs. "Never let it be said that I want to get in the way of your shenanigans with your husbands."

Clem blurts out, "I think you can do better than shenanigans. You've been around us far too long for such a tame word."

I reach over, swatting her arm. "Leave her alone," I snort.

"A little bam bam in the ham. Is that better?" Winnie giggles.

I roar out laughing. "Your son would die if he heard you say that."

"That's a good one," Clem hoots, slapping her knee.

"I think you've broken her, Clem." Margret cackles.

I look over at Ellie. "What are you doing?" She has her phone clutched in her hand.

"I'm texting Ian what she said. He'll get a kick out of it and come home horny."

"He's in a meeting with Ethan about the mayor position."

"Oh, good. Your husband will be horngry too."

"Ellie's been Googling dirty words again," Molly cackles.

"I'll have to write that one down. Horny and hungry," Clem makes a note in her phone.

"This went bad rather quickly," I snicker.

"I love it and wouldn't want it any other way," Winnie says.

CHAPTER THIRTY ONE

ROSE

"*I* can do this. I can raise a baby all on my own," I sniff, pacing the floor of my place. "I don't need him." I fall onto my bed. "But, I love him. I was envisioning our life together. Both of us growing the business, traveling together, creating a great life."

All this time I thought I'd go it alone. It felt good having a partner. The last eight weeks with him, working with him, I fell completely head over heels in love. "How could I have let myself do it? I was perfectly content being alone."

I change into my overalls and floppy hat and run down the stairs, hoping onto the mule. I drive out to the middle of the vineyard and pick a bucket of blueberries then head to the cellar. I can't walk in here anymore without thinking of Dodge.

"This is where you were created, little one." I pat my belly. "It wasn't what we planned, but I'm going to take care of you, don't you worry none." I check on all the barrels of wine and the batches of whiskey that are brewing. I have Dodge to thank for the success of Boone's Brand.

"That's what I'll do. I'll write him a check and tell him to move on," I say out loud.

"I don't want your money." Dodge is standing behind me.

I was so lost in my own mind, I didn't even hear him come down the stairs. "I don't rightly care what you want," I say, spinning on my heels.

"Please be quiet for once and let me talk."

I purse my lips together feeling angry.

"There was this woman in California. We started dating not long after I moved there. She worked for the same company I did. We worked on buying... stealing, as you'd say, a company out of New York. We spent a lot of time together. When the deal was to close, I wanted to ask her to move in with me. Turns out, she was using me to gain a foot up in the company. She convinced the seller to tell our boss that she did all the work to gain the commission, which was a pretty penny."

I soften at his story. "I'm sorry."

"Let me finish." He inhales. "Turns out she was pregnant with my child. I only found out because my best friend at the time overheard her talking to one of her girlfriends at the bar. She had no idea he was sitting behind her in a booth. He heard her tell her friend she was having an abortion. He felt I had the right to know."

I can't help but hold his hand.

"I went over to her apartment and confronted her. I begged her to have the baby, promising I'd take care of her and the baby."

"What happened?"

"She didn't want children with me or any other man. I tried to convince her to have it and I'd take sole responsibility and raise the child on my own."

"She wouldn't do it," I whisper the words as tears form in the corners of my eyes like his.

"No. I cried my heart out the day she aborted my child. I swore I'd never want another child in my life. It crushed me. I couldn't bear the idea of losing another child."

"This isn't the same, Dodge. We love each other. We may not have realized at the time he was

351

conceived, but he was created in love. It doesn't sound like you loved this woman."

"I cared for her, yes, but in the back of my mind there was always you. I'm sorry I needed time to get my head together. My reaction should've been totally happy. Given different past circumstances, it would've been, and for that I'm truly sorry."

"How do you feel now that you've had time to digest the fact that I'm pregnant?" I hold my breath, waiting for his answer.

He gets on his knees, placing his hands on my hips, with his gaze glued to my belly. "I love your mother with all my heart. I promise to love you just as much. You're not someone I knew I wanted, but you're exactly what I need." He glances up at me. "I promise to love you and this baby."

He stands and I hug him. "I love you, Dodge."

"I called Ian and told him to scrap the plans on tearing down the house. I want us to restore the old one and fill the rooms with our children." His lips meet mine with the softest kiss full of promise.

"Are you one hundred percent sure?"

"A hundred and ten percent. We might all have to live in this place until the house is done."

"I don't mind one bit."

"I'll work on finding a job so that I can support us."

"I've been thinking about that. I want you to work here with me. Together we can create the best vineyard in the world. I can't do it without you. I want us to be partners in everything we do. This place makes enough money to support us."

"That doesn't mean you'll be bossing me around does it?" he grins.

"I wouldn't be your boss, silly, but don't think for one minute I'm not going to make you pull your weight around here," I wink, teasing him.

"I love you, Rose, and this little one." His gaze trails down.

"I have one favor to ask when it comes to the baby." I lift his chin to look me in the eye.

"What's that?"

"If it's a boy, I want to name him Chet."

"I think there isn't any other name for him. If it's a girl, we're in a heap of trouble," he chuckles.

"Then we'd better hope for a boy, because a girl is going to have a tough time in life being called Chet Calhoun Anderson."

EPILOGUE

Clem

"*I*t's hard to believe our son is graduating high school. Wasn't it just yesterday he was born?"

Boone's large, rough hand rests in mine as we watch our baby receive his diploma. "The time has gone by way too fast," I sniff.

"We've done a good job. He's a smart, kind young man."

"I only wish Daddy was here to see it."

"Trust me, he's watching."

We hold on to each other as the ceremony

finishes, and my entire family meets back at the main house, just like we always have for any big events in our life. Our family has grown so much we have to set tables out back on the big porch in order for all of us to gather in one spot. Laughter and stories fill the air.

As I sit back and listen, my mind wanders through all the years of growing pains. We've had each other's backs from day one, even if we didn't know it. Life has changed so much since I came home all those years ago. Wyatt, who I struggled with, is one of my favorite people. He's a strong man with a loving heart. His ranch has flourished. He's the largest cattle owner in the state of Kentucky. His children have all grown up. Chase is married and starting a family of his own. Amelia took over the bed-and-breakfast when Margret and Jane stepped down. After several years of therapy, Margret walks on her own, something none of us ever thought she'd do again. She's an amazing woman. I have to chuckle, thinking how much I truly disliked her. Funny how things change. She's been a blessing in my life and a good friend.

Ellie and Ian have had issues over the years, but their bond seems stronger than ever. The children are all grown but live on the ranch. Ian's company grew so large he hired someone else to run it so he could spend more time with his family. Boone and I still see them sneaking off to skinny dip in the river. It does my heart good to see them still in love.

Bear and Nita are still going strong. They spend most of their time chasing the four grandchildren Missy and Tucker gave them. Their son has one of his own on its way. Missy won two Kentucky derbies and hung up her racing hat.

Noah and Molly have purchased up half of Salt Lick. Noah said it was his way of keeping the wolves at bay from trying to buy the ranch. Daddy would be proud of the way he's taken over the business. Molly and Jane have remained best friends.

Ethan and Jane are the couple I admire the most. They've been through so much together, yet the gleam in their eyes for one another has never faded. Ethan is the best person I know, and I'm proud to call him a friend after all these years. It's hard to believe Mercy will be the next to graduate. Their other two children they adopted are two years behind Mercy. The twin boys were brought to them when they were a year old. Their parents were killed in a car crash, leaving them orphans. It completed their family, and we all fell head over heels in love with them, including Winnie, who passed a few years ago. She rests on the mountain beside Momma and Daddy, right where she belongs.

Rose and Dodge are the jet-setters. They've traveled all over the world with the winery. They seem to have the best of both worlds. They treasure their time at home with Chet. I was always surprised they didn't have more children, but given how much they come and go, Rose said she didn't want to take any precious time away from her son. He's as well-traveled as they are. Dodge was the perfect man for Rose all along. She looks at him the way I still look at Boone.

He's the love of my life. I treasure everything about him, the good and the bad, just like he does for me. There is no other place in this world that I'd rather be than Whiskey River Road. It will always and forever be my home.

THANK YOU

Thank you so much for loving Whiskey River Road Series as much as I do. I appreciate it so much. The Vineyard is the last book in the series. I will be on to write something different, but may revisit a spinoff of Whiskey River Road in the future.

Make sure to check out my website and join my Newsletter for up to date information www.kellymooreauthor.com

If you love a Navy SEAL, you'll love The Fated Lives Series.

Available on Kindle, Paperback, and Audible.

Fated Lives Series

Rebel's Retribution Books 1-4. Audible

Theo's Retaliation Books 5-7. Audible

Thorn's Redemption Audible

Fallon's Revenge Book 11 Audible

Chapter One
Rebel

She wraps her firm leg around my hip and presses her core into my body, causing me to harden again despite a night of full-on sex. "Baby, you keep that up"—I look between my legs—"no pun intended, I'll never make the mission."

"God forbid you miss out on one mission." She unwinds her body from mine and throws the sheet off as she gets out of my bed. Her lean body and nice ass make for the perfect view.

"Come on, Ekko, and bring that fine ass back to bed."

"You know I hate when you call me that when we're not at work."

I fall back on the bed with a huff and rub my hand down my scruffy face. "Nina Pax, would you please crawl back into bed with me?" My team calls her Ekko because she's always in our ear over the coms, and when we disregard her orders, she repeats them over and over.

"I can't. I'm going to be late for my meeting with the commander," she says with a mouth full of toothpaste, waving her pink brush at me.

Groaning, I lift a leg up and hike myself out of bed, joining her in the bathroom. "You want me to skip out on a mission, but you're not willing to miss a meeting." I wrap my hands around her naked frame and press my teeth lightly into her shoulder.

"My life isn't on the line every time I go to work." She leans over and spits into the sink, pressing her ass into my dick. I place my hands on either side of her hips, then I smack her on the ass.

"Hey!" She laughs and turns in my arms. "You know how much I like your hands on me, but I really don't have time." She gives a quick kiss to my lips.

I reach for the shaving cream and lather it on my face. "When are you ever going to agree to marrying me?" I watch her reflection in the mirror as she dresses in her civilian black suit. She looks sexy as shit in it.

"We've talked about this. Neither one of our careers are good on marriages."

She's the handler for our SEAL Team Six Division, aka The Gunners. Everything about her is highly classified. She doesn't give much away, but I know her research of Afghanistan, and knowledge of tactical skills and weaponry, coupled with her negotiating skills, got her this job against some of the highest-ranking officers in the military. She even negotiated her way into staying a civilian rather than join the military. She wanted to be able to freelance her work to the highest bidder. She's brilliant and sexy. Killer combo.

I smooth the razor down my face as the shaving cream drips into the sink. "Why don't we both retire then?"

She sits on the small, rickety bench seat by the closet and slips on a pair of black shiny heels. "Neither one of us are ready for that. You love your job."

"I would give it up for you."

She gets up and stands beside me, looking at me in the mirror. "Derrick, I'm not ready to give any of this up. I have some things really starting to work for me." She winds her mocha-colored hair up into a bun.

I know when she calls me Derrick, she's serious. When we're in bed, she cries out my last name, Rebel. That's me, Captain Derrick Rebel. Leader of the SEAL Team Six Division. "I have no idea what that means. Everything you do turns out gold. You've gotten us out of more shit than any military leader I've had in the past."

"My lips are sealed." She smacks them together, spreading on her nude-colored lipstick.

"I know, highly classified, need to know only." I rinse off my face and towel dry before I grab her to me. "The only thing I need to know is that you love me." I kiss the tip of her nose.

"You know I do. Now please take your sexy ass back to bed and skip this mission. Let Captain Stark step in for you today. He'll be jonesing to go out on standby for you."

"Fat chance of that, and let him take all the glory? These are my men and the only way I'm not leading them is if I'm six feet under." Some emotion crosses her face, but I'm not sure what it is.

She squeezes her eyes closed and presses the palm of her hand against her temple. "Ahh...I really gotta go." She turns to leave, but I see her glance back in my direction. "I'll see you in the war room, Rebel." Her smile is gone, and her eyes look sad.

"You okay?"

"Yeah. Good luck on your mission today."

She cracks open the door and slinks out of my barracks. She's only fooling herself thinking others don't know about us. My men called it the first time I laid eyes on her. She came into the camp's gym to work out in a pair of gray shorts and a white tank top. She had more muscles in her arms than some of the men.

She got on the pull-up bar, and I couldn't take my eyes off her. One of my men yelled out that he thought she could do more pull-ups than me. The challenge was real. She almost kicked my butt. I couldn't let her show me up. I pulled a bicep muscle rather than lose. I kept doing them despite the pain that was burning up my arm.

She was pretty pissed off, and my peace offering was a beer in the barrack's cantina. Her smart mouth and sexy lips had me hard the entire night, which led to me fucking her brains out. She was a tiger in bed, leaving scratches down my back. I think it was her way of paying me back for beating her in front of the men. I'd do it all over again to feel her nails dig into my skin from pure pleasure.

I open my closet door and take my fatigues off the hanger and pull out a white T-shirt from a drawer. I'm married to these clothes. I joined the Navy right out of high school. It was the only thing I ever wanted to do—to follow in my grandfather's footsteps. Now, at thirty-three, I wouldn't mind settling down and having a few kids running around. Even if I convinced Nina to marry me, she's made it pretty clear that she has no room in her life for children. It's not in the grand scheme of her life plan. She's very regimented and never flies by the seat of her pants.

Unlike me, I'm a hardcore rule breaker, and it drives Nina insane. My theory is, sometimes you have to break the rules to make things work. We've gotten in more knock-down, drag-out fights than I'd like to think about after a mission because I ignored Ekko in my ear. But damn, it was worth the make-up sex.

As I lace up my boots, a video pops up on my laptop with my older brother's face on it. "Hey, bro, you there?"

I slide into the chair in front of the small desk. "Hey, Sean. What's up? I only have a minute or so to talk."

"I wanted you to know I got the loan for the bar

and you and the boys will have a place to celebrate when you come back home to Portland."

"Congrats, man. I'm happy for you. Did you pick a name for it?" I lean back on two legs of the chair.

"Sean's place." He's all smiles.

"Real original, man." I chuckle. How about Rebel's Bar."

"That would give you some claim to it, and you aren't getting your SEAL hands on it." He laughs. "You protect the country, I'll serve the beer."

"How are Mom and Dad?"

"Enjoying their retirement by traveling the world."

I glance at my black military watch. "I gotta go, man. Tell Mom and Dad I love them the next time you talk to them."

"Will do."

"Congrats again, Sean. Drink a couple for me."

Grabbing my gear and pulling on my hat, I run out the door and down the two steps to the dirty, hot ground of our platoon.

"Hey, Cap."

"Good morning, Barker." The lieutenant steps in pace with me. He's the oldest member in our team of eight.

"I hear we're going in dark on our mission to capture the leader of the MM20 group."

I pull my bag farther up on my shoulder. "Let's go find out."

To Continue Rebel's Retribution Books 1-4. Audible

ABOUT THE AUTHOR

.

"This author has the magical ability to take an already strong and interesting plot and add so many unexpected twists and turns that it turns her books into a complete addiction for the reader." Dandelion Inspired Blog

www.kellymooreauthor.com

Armed with books in the crook of my elbow, I can go anywhere. That's my philosophy! Better yet, I'll write the books that will take me on an adventure.

My heroes are a bit broken but will make you swoon. My heroines are their own kick-ass characters armed with humor and a plethora of sarcasm.

If I'm not tucked away in my writing den, with coffee firmly gripped in hand, you can find me with a book propped on my pillow, a pit bull lying across my legs, a Lab on the floor next to me, and two kittens running amuck.

My current adventure has me living in Idaho with my own gray-bearded hero, who's put up with my shenanigans for over thirty years, and he doesn't mind all my book boyfriends.

If you love romance, suspense, military men, lots of action and adventure infused with emotion, tear-worthy moments, and laugh-out-loud humor, dive into my books and let the world fall away at your feet.

ALSO BY KELLY MOORE

Whiskey River Road Series - Available on Audible

Coming Home, Book 1

Stolen Hearts, Book 2

Three Words, Book 3

Kentucky Rain, Book 4

Wild Ride, Book 5

Magnolia Mill, Book 6

Rough Road, Book 7

Lucky Man, Book 8

Simple Man, Book 9

The Vineyard, Book 10

The Broken Pieces Series in order

Broken Pieces

Pieced Together

Piece by Piece

Pieces of Gray

Syn's Broken Journey

Broken Pieces Box set Books 1-3

August Series in Order

Next August

This August

Seeing Sam

The Hitman Series- Previously Taking Down Brooklyn/The DC Seres

Stand By Me - On Audible as Deadly Cures

Stay With Me On Audible as Dangerous Captive

Hold Onto Me

Epic Love Stories Series can be read in any order

Say You Won't Let Go. Audiobook version

Fading Into Nothing Audiobook version

Life Goes On. Audiobook version

Gypsy Audiobook version

Jameson Wilde Audiobook version

Rescue Missions Series can be read in any order

Imperfect. On Audible

Blind Revenge

Fated Lives Series

Rebel's Retribution Books 1-4. Audible